A SHADOW OF HOPE

A Shadow of Hope

The Story of Dr. Samuel A. Mudd

Pamela Bauer Mueller

Piñata Publishing

Piñata Publishing
626 Old Plantation Road
Jekyll Island, GA 31527
(912) 635-9402
www.pinatapub.com

Library of Congress Cataloging-in-Publication Data

Names: Bauer Mueller, Pamela. author.
Title: A shadow of hope : Dr. Samuel Mudd 1864-1871 / Pamela Bauer Mueller.

Published/Produced Jekyll Island, GA : Pinata Publishing, [2018]

Includes bibliographical references.

Identifiers: LCCN 2017010101 | ISBN 9780980916355 (pbk.)

Subjects: LCSH: Mudd, Samuel Alexander, 1833-1883—Fiction.
| LCGFT: Historical fiction. | Biographical fiction.

Classification: LCC PS3602.A93566 S53 2018 | DDC 813/.6—DC23
LC record available at https://lccn.loc.gov2017010101

Cover art by Gini Steele
Cover photo by John Nicholas Fuechsel
Typeset by Vancouver Desktop Publishing Centre
Printed and bound in the United States by Cushing-Malloy, Inc.

To Phyllis Bauer—my mother, my inspiration.
Thank you for who you are.

Pray about everything; tell God your needs and don't forget to thank Him for His answers. If you do this you will experience God's peace ... His peace will keep your thoughts and your hearts quiet and at rest.
—Philippians 4: 6-7

Optimism is the faith that leads to achievement. Nothing can be done without hope and confidence.
—Helen Keller

AUTHOR'S NOTE

The art of writing is almost an act of hypnosis. I feel extremely challenged when I begin each book. This past year was especially difficult because our lives became a series of disruptions and distractions. The negative propaganda of the presidential election was beating at us from all sides. In October, Hurricane Matthew raged through coastal Georgia and forced our family and cats to evacuate on short notice. Over the next four days on the road, I decided to begin writing this manuscript.

Two weeks later we lost Sukey Spice, our beloved calico cat, to cancer. I spent a few days in mourning and then returned to Dr. Samuel Mudd's life story.

Dr. Mudd's bravery, love and resilience truly touched my heart, and also inspired me to look beyond our situation and share his story. His unwitting assistance to the disguised assassin of President Lincoln proved the adage that *no good deed goes unpunished*. Innocent, he was still convicted and imprisoned in Fort Jefferson, where he endured brutal punishments and appalling conditions.

History is a conversation between the present and the past: a story tied up with language, conflict, settings and characters. The author's task is to sharpen her narrative line with compelling dialog that brings it to life, using credible characters.

Strong characterization is critical; paying close attention to your people and the action swirling around them will advance the story logically and memorably. Depicting characters with careful attention and heart is the novelist's prerogative—and obligation.

Dialog had to be created, although every effort was made to base it on the character's personality, temperament and education. I dove deeply into memoirs, diaries, countless letters and published accounts by relatives, friends, associates and even enemies.

On a deeper level, I needed to imagine the emotional truths that drove each of them to act in a certain way.

Writing is also a mixture of instinct and intention, of creative impulse and painstaking research and revision. I believe the story must work on a superficial level, as a simple narrative, but also on a deeper level to satisfy readers looking back to revisit certain passages. A reader's mind should be enticed to discover all the nuances of a story.

Because I write non-fiction historical novels, I must combine journalism with the literary liberties of some fictional dialog. Often I used the "written words" of the characters' journals, letters, etc. and turned them into the "spoken words" in the dialogs. Every character and event in this book is real—with the exception of the turtle Liberty, who fit in so well I gave him his own identity.

I only played with the timeline on two occasions to help the narrative flow more smoothly. Every novel will slow or speed up time, fast-forward or reverse it, and make a scene as precise as today's news or as wispy as a distant memory. And the book you are holding is no exception.

As always, I conducted extensive research before

bringing you this tale. In order to understand him better, I visited the Mudd farm in Maryland and his grave in the local church cemetery, and then trudged through the rugged swamp into which John Wilkes Booth escaped after Dr. Mudd set his broken leg.

My husband and I visited the Ford Theater in Washington D.C., to visualize the tension on the fateful night of President Lincoln's assassination. I interviewed everyone I could find who knew or had information about Dr. Samuel Mudd.

The first research trip for this story was to the Dry Tortugas, where I walked all over the island and through Fort Jefferson; then experienced the cell where Dr. Mudd languished for almost four years. As with all my novels, I dedicated eight to ten months to digging into the heart and soul of my main character.

In my case, the greatest happiness is not knowing exactly where I am going with all this research. I love the feeling of waking up and thinking about my characters, the next moment in their lives, or the next bend in some high and nameless road. The exhilarating adventure of exploring the unknown has always been a primary motivation to write another book. And writing brings me deep personal peace.

I believe in a certain amount of "luck," but I do not believe luck got me where I am, any more than it explains Dr. Mudd's trials and tribulations. Hard work and God's hand have made it all happen for me, along with unshakable values and striving to do the right thing.

My father taught me that I could do anything if I set my mind to it and was true to myself. I've encountered many obstacles in life and moved past them; picked myself up again after every tumble. I've learned to speak my mind without being intimidated by critics or demoralized by negativity.

Being myself is a great gift God has given to me. But the greatest gift is His grace.

PROLOGUE

JULY 24, 1865

A tall white lighthouse towered menacingly over the tropical island's thin fringe of palm trees. It was mid-afternoon; we were sailing through the winding channel and slowly approaching the island. The sunlight glaring through the blue-gray sky wasn't bright enough to burn off air so thick it seemed to dim the island's natural colors. Big-chested frigate birds wheeled and danced through the sky above us; white sandy beaches and deep green trees almost hid a thin brick-red line—the moat's seawall—and behind it about thirteen acres of brick fortress. Azure waters seemed to stretch forever as still as a pool in a deep cavern, so pristine and clear we might be able to identify colorful objects buried in sand fathoms below.

"Don't suppose we'll be seeing any of this after today," Spangler muttered. "I wonder how miserable our quarters will be."

Just before docking, the water grew shallower and our gunboat drifted over what might have been an ocean garden. Schools of multi-colored fish darted in and out among huge heads of coral reef in perfect freedom. Sea ferns swayed with the tide as if welcoming us grimly to

Fort Jefferson: America's largest military prison.

My eyes absorbed the particulars of the fortress: a forbidding three-story structure topped with earthworks and ammunition bunkers. A wide moat skirted one of the fort walls; brick and mortar lined the side and ran around the two bastions in front. Eels played hide and seek around the boat docks' pylons.

Fort Jefferson had been built in the Dry Tortugas, a cluster of seven Caribbean islands some seventy miles west of Key West, Florida that included my new "home" on Garden Key. The reason the islands were called "Dry" would soon become painfully clear.

Just then our boat's signal gun blasted close by, almost knocking me off my feet. Immediately the fort's commander acknowledged our arrival with his own cannon.

Spangler, O'Laughlen and Arnold stood nearby looking equally desolate. I could not suppress a cynical smile about what a miserable figure our group of pale landlubbers was cutting—a doctor, a carpenter, a feed store clerk and a commissary worker.

The Fort's duty officer was rowed out to our gunboat to accompany us to shore. Just as we prepared to change vessels, a sudden tropical storm split the heavens open and drenched us all. The palm trees flattened out against the sky like exotic umbrellas, rocking irritably on their tall, narrow stalks. Cutting winds whipped and soaked our light clothing as we struggled to disembark.

Jagged lightning forked toward us, pungent with the odor of ozone. Thunder bellowed overhead. As my eyes looked toward the grim, foreboding citadel, a sense of

impending doom nearly suffocated me. I was now officially a hostage, restrained by thick walls and a moat built
specifically to keep enemies out and prisoners in.

PART ONE

1

APRIL 14, 1865

Ford's Theatre is brilliantly illuminated; everyone is happy. They have gathered to celebrate the imminent end of a war that had caused so much desolation and bloodshed. It is a priceless opportunity for the good-hearted leader who has suffered a thousand agonies to bask in the respect and admiration of his beloved people. A peaceful smile—not seen since the beginning of the war—beams down as the theater company prepares to entertain its benefactor.

It is Good Friday, April 14, 1865. The play is *Our American Cousin*. His wife had encouraged him to attend, only hours before, enticing him with a little historical vignette.

"Do you remember, my darling, that this theatrical performance was playing in Chicago the day you were nominated to be the presidential candidate?"

He smiles tenderly at her. "I certainly do, my dear. And I am happy to accompany you to this performance. We will celebrate that day, among our many other blessings."

The theater's lead usher—a portly gentleman with bushy mutton chops—meets them at the entryway and escorts them to their box.

"It is a rare privilege to have you with us this evening, Sir," he says with a bow. "I'm certain you can use a respite from years of inestimable service to our nation."

Several hours later, a thin man steps through the stage door and strides through the backstage, around the pulley ropes and sets. After a final glimpse into the backstage mirror to straighten his waistcoat, he greets several friends before pushing through the outer door of a corridor that leads to the President's box. He slowly forces it open and wedges a piece of wood against the door.

Taking a half dozen quick steps, he reaches the doorway of the President's box and peers through a hole drilled earlier to check the President's position. He enters quietly and pauses three feet behind the President. It is 10:15 p.m.

He steps softly out of the shadows, a small Derringer in his right hand and a knife in his left. No one has seen him; no one knows he is there. The President has chosen this exact moment to lean forward, turning his head slightly to the left to peer down and savor this moment with the audience. He feels grateful that he was able to bring America back from the brink of apocalypse by holding fast to his faith in God and the Union.

The gunman, knowing at exactly which moment the audience will chuckle at a comical line, aims carefully at the fold behind his target's left ear and squeezes the trigger. The pistol kicks as a ball burrows into the President's brain through a round hole in his skull. After a split-second snap of pain, the President senses nothing more.

His wife, confused to see a stranger in the box with them, stops laughing when her husband slumps forward across the balustrade. Major Henry Reed Rathbone whips around at the sound of the tiny gunshot and jumps to his feet. Behind the puff of smoke, he sees a man crouched between the door and the President and immediately strikes a defensive pose. The shooter drops the Derringer, transferring the knife into his gun hand as Major Rathbone vaults toward him.

Raising the knife to shoulder level, the shooter brings it down in a hacking motion as Rathbone throws up his left arm in defense. The Major can feel the blade slicing through the skin and biceps of his left arm, down to the bone.

Mary stifles a scream and covers her mouth with trembling hands, her eyes widening in stark terror. The shooter pushes his body in front of her, screaming the word "Freedom" at the audience. The shout is barely heard over the rising mayhem below.

Swinging his legs over the balustrade, he drops twelve feet. A gymnastic leap onto the stage has become almost routine for this veteran thespian. But on this twelve-foot drop he misjudges the thickness of the massive United States flag decorating the front of the box.

His right spur tangles in the flag's folds and ruins his two-footed landing on the stage. Dropping awkwardly to the boards, he braces his left foot and both hands to catch his fall. He hears and then feels his fibula snap. Later he would be thankful for the tight boot which will now serve as a splint.

Momentarily stunned, he stares at the blood-smeared dagger still clutched in his right hand. Above him the man he just shot slumps forward as if asleep. The production's lead actor, Harry Hawk, is standing nearby at center stage, bewildered and confused by the other actor's sudden cameo appearance. Time stops for all players in this historic scene.

Then the shooter drags himself up onto one knee, madly slashing the long knife through the air and shouting, "The South shall be free!" Facing the audience, from center stage for his final appearance, he bellows, "Sic semper tyrannis" (*thus always to tyrants*), as Harry Hawk runs off the stage.

Shaking his head to clear it, the shooter staggers and limps off the stage. Chaos shakes the theater as the audience surges to its feet and pushes toward the exits. Some women faint. Many others are trapped in the confusion and turmoil.

"Stop that man!" screams Major Rathbone from the box, standing near the balustrade and bleeding profusely.

"The President has been shot," yells Clara Harris, Rathbone's fiancée, helping him stay on his feet. "Help us, please!"

The shooter hobbles to the rear stage door just ahead of the set carpenter Ritterspaugh. They reach the exit at the same moment, but Ritterspaugh leaps back when he sees the knife. This brief pause allows the shooter to squeeze through the door into the alley, grab his horse's reins from the boy holding them, and lift himself up into the saddle.

In the bedlam that follows, a doctor probes the President's gaping wound and rises unsteadily to his feet. Wiping away tears, he quietly tells the men in the room to carry the President to the boardinghouse across the street.

The moon lights up the sky. The agitated horse appears to circle from left to right in a quick zigzag, its rider crouching forward over the pommel. When a spontaneous torchlight parade blocks his planned getaway onto Tenth Street, he swerves into a back alley and spurs his horse in another direction, turning on F Street.

Grinning wickedly, the shooter disappears into the night.

2

APRIL 15, 1865

Booth arrived at the Navy Yard Bridge to cross Anacostia Creek at approximately 10:45 p.m. Challenged by the guard, he gave his correct name and his correct destination—Beantown, Maryland. He was not wearing a disguise.

"Are you unaware that the rules allow no persons to pass after nine o'clock at night?" asked the sentry.

"No, Sir, I did not know that. I am on my way home to Beantown. May I please continue?" The sentry, after careful consideration, waved him across. Booth forced his tired horse up the long, steep hill of Anacostia, where he finally rested and waited for Herold.

A second rider galloped up to the bridge on a medium-sized roan horse and gave a false name and destination. He lied about overstaying his visit in the city, admitting he knew the curfew was at 9:00 p.m. Like the first rider, Herold posed no threat by leaving the city and was allowed to continue.

A third rider approached and was stopped. He gave his name as John Fletcher, and he told the sentry he had come to the city to recover his stolen horse from the thief Davy Herold. He was informed that a man of Herold's description had just passed over the bridge and if he pursued him, he could not return until the following morning. A tired and dispirited Fletcher decided to return to the city.

David Herold caught up with Booth atop Bryantown Road and they rode fast, arriving in southern Maryland around 11:00 p.m. Booth was beside himself with excitement.

"I have struck a mortal blow at the heart of the United States!" he proclaimed in his most stentorian voice.

"Do you still believe it was wise to assassinate rather than kidnap him?" his companion asked.

"Certainly. This will create havoc that nobody but Lincoln could overcome!"

They dismounted at the Surratt Tavern in Surrattsville about midnight.

John Harrison Surratt Sr.'s widow, Mary, had first leased the tavern to John M. Lloyd after her husband's death. Since then it had become a "safe house" along the Confederate underground route from Richmond to Washington. The two riders asked to see manager John Lloyd. When he finally appeared, he was clearly inebriated and slightly annoyed at being bothered at that hour.

"For God's sake, Lloyd, make haste and get those things we need," demanded Herold. Mary Surratt had arranged for some supplies to be delivered earlier that afternoon.

The manager returned with two Spencer carbines, ammunition, Booth's field glasses and two bottles of whiskey. He handed the carbines up to Booth, noticing how difficult it was for the actor to remain balanced on his horse with both guns. Booth realized that too and reluctantly handed one carbine back. "Keep it," he told Lloyd.

Wheeling their horses around, they galloped away into the darkness.

"We have assassinated the President and Secretary Seward," shouted Booth, guzzling whiskey as they disappeared.

Lloyd would be arrested the following week and questioned by Officer George Cottingham at Roby's Post Office, near Surrattsville. He wept bitterly, threw his arms around his wife, and called for his prayer book. Before long he began describing how John H. Surratt Jr., Atzerodt and Herold had left the carbines at his place. He told officers how Mrs. Surratt had come to his place on the afternoon of the assassination and requested that the supplies, including two bottles of whiskey, be held in readiness for the parties who would call for them that night.

"And where is the carbine that Booth left behind?" Cottingham asked him.

"It is upstairs, in a little room where Mrs. Surratt keeps some bags."

It was found behind the plastering of the wall in a large bag, suspended by a string tied around the muzzle. Only the best-trained eye would recognize that the wall had recently been re-painted. By the time they discovered it, the string had broken and the carbine had fallen down between the cracks.

Meanwhile, Herold and Booth put spurs to the horses and rode at breakneck speed toward their freedom, awaiting them across the Potomac in Virginia. Booth's broken leg began to throb so painfully he knew it needed immediate medical attention. That made him think of the gentlemanly Dr. Mudd, whom he had met the previous November. He knew that Dr. Mudd's farm was only a few miles away, just off the highway.

Herold wanted to keep riding toward safety, but Booth insisted he needed medical attention. So the exhausted Herold nudged his horse behind Booth through a maze of back country roads to their second stop, the home of the Southern sympathizer Dr. Samuel A. Mudd. At this point the broken bone in Booth's leg was beginning to lacerate his flesh.

By the time the weary riders reached the white frame farmhouse, the Mudd family had been asleep for hours.

3

April 15, 1865

My wife and I were dragged rudely from slumber at around 4:00 a.m. by a sharp knock on our bedroom window. As I rolled from the bed to pull on my trousers, the knocking had become a muted thumping on the front door. As a country physician, I am accustomed to facing emergencies, but rarely at such an ungodly hour.

Outside the door, I could barely make out my two young visitors: one sat tall in the saddle while the other had dismounted and was holding the horses. I did not recognize either of them and asked their business.

Without any apology for the late hour, the man on foot replied, "We just came in from St. Mary's Company, on our way to Washington City. A few miles back my friend's horse slipped and fell on him, breaking his leg."

Lifting my candle higher, I could see enough to realize the friend was in serious distress and needed prompt medical assistance. "Come inside," I said, "and let's position you on the sofa."

I used large shears to cut the boot from his leg and foot, longitudinally in front of the instep. I set it aside and quickly examined the leg. I found a direct fracture about two inches above the ankle joint.

Although it wasn't a compound injury, I wanted to treat him on a bed, so his friend and I carried him upstairs. As we lifted him to the bed, I noticed the patient's slim and rather athletic physique.

"Please attend to the injury quickly so we can continue our journey to Washington," pleaded the younger one who did the speaking. "We must make haste."

Assuring them I understood their urgency, I attended the injured man.

I observed he had a strange-looking beard, as well as a wrap around his head to cover his face. He did not remove it during my treatment.

I pushed the protruding bone back into place and joined the two bones as securely as possible by cutting up an old band box and fashioning it into a splint.

After finishing my work, I suggested they both rest in the guest room until daylight. But the young companion was restless. To give my patient a few minutes so the pain might subside, I invited the other man to take a walk with me around the farm while I fed the animals.

"What is your name?" I asked him.

"Henson."

"And your friend?"

"His name is Tyser," he muttered, avoiding eye contact.

My wife served us breakfast; then Henson asked if he could borrow a razor to shave off his friend's moustache. I fetched one from my kit with a pitcher of water and a wash basin. My wife cleaned the upstairs hall while Henson shaved Tyser's moustache. She tapped on the guest room door.

"Do you need anything else?" she asked with her customary friendly smile. A moment later Henson opened the door half way to answer.

"No, Ma'am. Thank you just the same."

Back downstairs she told me it seemed Tyser's chin whiskers had come loose while his moustache was being shaved. Having had a chance to look at those whiskers while setting his leg, I wondered aloud if they were real.

Sometime later, when I went upstairs to check on him, I saw that although the moustache had disappeared, he still had the mysterious long whiskers.

Henson closed the bedroom door behind him and leaned exhausted against the door frame. I knew just how he felt.

"Tyser will need another way to travel. Do you know where we might find some type of wagon?"

After our mid-day meal of chicken and collard greens, Mr. Henson and I rode over to my father Henry's Oak Hill farm to inquire about a carriage or wagon. He was away and my brother told us that there was nothing available. I had several other errands to attend to so I agreed to accompany Henson into town.

The village of Bryantown is about five miles south of my farm. Approaching the town center, Henson suddenly explained that he wanted to check on his friend and turned his horse back toward my house. The town seemed to be buzzing with knots of people engaged in serious discussions, chatting and gesturing with soldiers everywhere. While purchasing nails, calico and pepper at the grocery store, I heard some terrible news.

"What is happening in the village? Why are so many standing around?"

"Have you not heard?" retorted the shop owner. "The president has been assassinated."

"What? By whom?" I responded, shocked and upset.

"Dunno, but it happened at Ford's Theatre last night."

My heart lurched. President Lincoln dead? Who could have killed our president? I had my differences with President Lincoln, but no one I knew could applaud such a violent act.

I rode home at a faster clip, now concerned about having strangers in my home with my wife and children. My neighbor Francis Farrell's farm was on the way so I made a brief stop to get further news about the assassination. John Hardy was standing in Farrell's yard and told me the killer's name was John Booth.

"John Wilkes Booth?" I asked. "The same one who was in the area last fall?"

Neither man was certain, as there were three or four men named Booth in the vicinity.

My heart tightened like a fist. Just a few months back, I had met an actor named John Wilkes Booth who had expressed interest in purchasing my property after a mutual friend introduced us. He did stop by the farm to see my property but never returned.

Hurrying to reach my house as I digested the news, I saw the two men mounting their horses, ready to depart.

It was about 5 p.m. and I thought it was an odd time to resume their journey.

"How are you feeling?" I asked my patient, watching him anxiously pull his head shawl more tightly over his face. "Are you ready to travel?"

His eyes conveyed the pain he was experiencing. "Good enough to get goin'," he lied. "Which way is it to Parson Wilmer's?"

As Tyser listened to my description of the most direct route, Henson rode some seventy yards ahead, fidgeting in the saddle and looking nervously down the road. I wished Tyser well with a handshake before he spurred his horse into a canter with his good leg. They hurried towards Zekiah Swamp, away from Bryantown and the 13th New York Cavalry.

Good Lord, I thought. *Who are these men?* I stood quietly for a long moment, mulling the possible answers. When Mr. Tyser had shaken my hand his head covering had fallen away, giving me a glimpse of his beardless chin. *Had he removed the whisker attachment now that his disguise would no longer be necessary?* The cold, clear reality of his identity swept over me and I struggled to breathe.

My heart buffeted around in my chest, hammering wildly. I took in long, deep breaths, trying to find my equilibrium. *Had I just set the broken leg of John Wilkes Booth—the actor who murdered our president?*

4

APRIL 22, 1865

Since their departure on April 15, my wife Frank (who was baptized Sarah) had become greatly concerned. She had realized the man's beard was false when he was hobbling downstairs and it became partially dislodged.

"Sammy, that man's beard was false, and I wonder why he wore it," she announced.

"I believe you, my dear. Here's what I learned earlier today in Bryantown. Based on the facts we must decide if that was John Wilkes Booth." I shared everything I had heard, as well as my own suspicions.

She nodded gravely and frowned. "Sam, you must return to Bryantown and raise the alarm."

I couldn't hide my sense of dread. "What if they return and find you alone with the children?"

"Then I shall accompany you to Sunday Mass tomorrow and we will tell them together," she decided.

The following morning we attended St. Peter's Catholic Church and sat with my cousin George Mudd. After so many hours reviewing the previous day's events, I felt overcome with anxiety, especially about my interactions with the injured man.

After mass I stopped George by the rear sacristy.

"George, have they apprehended Lincoln's killer yet?" I asked uneasily.

"No, Sam. I think not."

I meticulously explained the previous night's encounter, adding a description of my two suspicious visitors. He advised me to tell the authorities everything forthwith.

"George," I explained uneasily, "because I was the doctor involved, yet oblivious of both men's identities, I hope you can make the report on my behalf."

He squeezed my shoulder, assuring me that he would. The next afternoon he stopped by the farm and shared his report.

"I spoke with Lieutenant Dana of the 13th New York Volunteer Cavalry about your visitors. I told them one had a broken leg and how you set it, having no idea of his identity. Even if you had known, we all realize that you had the professional duty to attend to him. I then insisted that you could never have considered him a fugitive or an assassin since you were unaware of President Lincoln's assassination."

He paused, concern clouding his eyes. "I went on to tell them that when you were told about the assassination by the famous actor John Wilkes Booth, you swore to me that you did not recognize this fugitive behind false whiskers and with his face covered. I said they had told you their names were Henson and Tyser, and you had no reason to believe otherwise."

I nodded soberly. "You did well, George. Did they believe you?"

He smiled and shrugged. "I think so, but they want to send out several detectives to visit you tomorrow. Just to ask more questions. I told them I thought that would be fine."

On Tuesday morning, April 18th, Lieutenant Alexander Lovett rode up followed by a team of detectives, searching for the assassin. They included William Williams, Joshua Lloyd and Simon Gavacan. George Mudd was told about the meeting and came to accompany my wife and me.

Lovett dismounted and introduced himself. They wanted to question Frank and me separately so we went into different rooms. Then Lovett asked me to tell him the whole story from the beginning; he listened closely and occasionally interrupted.

"Did you recognize either one of the men?"

"No Sir, I did not. They were complete strangers whom I had never seen before and knew nothing about." I described them both, adding that the injured one's friend asked for a razor to shave off the other one's moustache. I added helpfully, "On reflection, that seems suspicious, but at the time I was too concerned about his medical status to worry about it."

"Describe him to me," he instructed, ignoring my comment.

"He had a moustache and rather long chin whiskers. And he spoke very little."

"When did you hear about President Lincoln's assassination?"

"On Sunday morning, in church." *Why am I so frightened to tell them I learned about it even before that?*

Lieutenant Lovett frowned as if he knew better. "What kind of horses were they riding? Did they say where they had been or where they were going?"

I nodded. "When they arrived at my farm they said

they were going to Washington City. Tyser, I think his name was, had had an accident when his horse fell on him, breaking a bone near his ankle."

I scratched my head and continued. "When they left, they wanted to know the most direct route to Parson Wilmer's house, near Piney Church. So I told them."

"Show us the path they took," Lovett said, rising abruptly. "How badly was the leg broken? Was it painful for him to ride?" I told them I imagined it was painful.

I led the search party to the edge of Zekiah Swamp. "This is the path I pointed out to them, but I did not actually remain outside my house to see them ride into the swamp."

The men plowed back and forth through the quagmire and tangled vegetation, five or six times. They traced the hoof-prints and looked for clues proving the men had indeed passed that way.

Finally, they departed. "Thank you for your help, Dr. Mudd. If we have more questions, we will return."

For the next few days Frank and I continued our daily routine as best we could. I went back and forth over every detail of the strangers' visit, fighting my deep-seated conviction that the injured man was John Wilkes Booth.

On Friday, April 21st, the search team returned, greeted Frank and told her that they were here to conduct a search. I was dining with my father's family at his farm, so Frank sent a servant to fetch me.

"Good afternoon, gentlemen," I addressed them, walking briskly through the entrance to my house. "How may I assist you?"

Lieutenant Lovett's friendly and polite demeanor had disappeared.

"We intend to search your house to see if you are hiding anything from us," he declared solemnly.

"I have nothing to hide, so you may look anywhere you wish." Wishing to be as cooperative as possible, I added. "I do have something you may be interested in."

Calling Frank, I asked her to please bring down the boot she had found after the strangers' departure.

She handed Lieutenant Lovett the riding boot I had cut off the bearded man's swollen ankle. "My wife found this under the bed he slept in. I had forgotten all about it."

Lieutenant Lovett scowled as he accepted the boot, peeling back the sliced leather. "There is some writing here, right here, along the inner top edge," he announced. It says, *Henry Lutz, maker, 445 Broadway, New York, J. Wilkes.*"

Darting a distrustful look at me, he inquired, "Had you seen this?"

I shook my head. "No, I had no reason to look that closely."

"Why did you not tell me about the false whiskers the last time we spoke?" he prodded.

"Sir, I believe I told you about his long chin whiskers, and I..."

"You did not, Dr. Mudd. It was your wife Sarah who told us."

I turned to her in a state of bewilderment. "Did we not mention that together, dear?"

Flustered, fearful that she had incriminated me in some way, she clarified. "I told these gentlemen that as the two strangers were leaving that afternoon, I took notice when the injured one came to the foot of the stairs, because his chin whiskers became detached. I believed they were false whiskers."

I smiled warmly at her, and she relaxed a little. "Yes, I thought so too. Perhaps I forgot to mention it to you, but I did tell George that before he met with you the first time."

"Indeed you did, cousin." George added, a bit annoyed at Lovett's inference.

"Well then, is there now any doubt in your mind that the man you treated is John Wilkes Booth?" probed Lovell. He leaned forward and pinned me with his scowl.

I felt my face flush as I quietly answered him. "No, Sir, I believe that is who I treated."

"And you knew him, correct?"

I felt panic blooming inside me and pushing all the air out of my lungs. I tried to sort out what this could mean. I hadn't anticipated such a hostile interrogation.

"I'm not certain, Sir. I think not. But as I said, I could not see his features because he hid them from us."

Lovett's eyes bored through me. He folded his arms over his chest.

"You will now come with me to Bryantown for more questioning, where I will hand you over to Colonel Wells." Turning to my wife, he tipped his hat. "Good day, Madam."

Frank reached out to me, and I held her close. Her gaze clung to mine, eyes rounded with vulnerability.

"Are you arresting Sam, Lieutenant Lovell?" she asked unsteadily.

He smiled unpleasantly. "No, Ma'am, but I admit I came here with that intention."

5

JULY 29, 1865

We were taken to Fort Jefferson under a cloak of secrecy. Everyone, including Frank, learned of the prisoner transfer from newspaper reports published after we were at sea. The government must have wanted to prevent anyone from attempting to free us through a writ of habeas corpus in case the assassination was part of a larger conspiracy.

We were told that construction of Fort Jefferson started in 1846 and would eventually use sixteen million imported bricks. After defending American waters from Caribbean pirates, the Fort prevented Confederate ships from entering the Gulf of Mexico. A seawater moat and drawbridge guarded the sally port, the fortress's single entrance outside the massive walls.

The Fort was still under construction when we arrived. We quickly joined the other prison laborers (mostly military deserters or civilian thieves) to continue working on the three-tiered, six-sided 420 heavy-gun Fort set with arched ports of "casemates." We mostly evacuated the moat or repaired masonry.

Two of its sides measured 325 feet; the other four sides measured 477 feet. The Army also employed civilian machinists, blacksmiths, carpenters, general laborers, masons and even slaves to help build the Fort. After 1863, slaves were no longer used.

By this time the island's military population had begun to decline and numbered 1,729. Residents included a civilian doctor and his family, a lighthouse keeper with his family, and several cooks with families. After the war, its 2,000 residents had been reduced to 1,088, including 531 enlisted soldiers and civilians, 30 officers and 527 prisoners. The Army had already transformed the fortress into a prison. Vacant casemates had become open-air cells for over 500 inmates serving time for desertion, mutiny, murder and other offenses.

We were placed in a gun casement and lectured on the prisoners' rules and regulations by the officer in charge. He warned us that if we misbehaved, we would be moved to a dark and desolate dungeon. He took us there to see it for ourselves. We read the inscription above the door reading: "Abandon all hope, you who enter here."

The group of prisoners from Maryland—Michael O'Laughlen, Sam Arnold, Edman (Ned) Spangler and I—shared a cell. We had an unobstructed view of the central parade ground and the comings and goings of the Fort's inhabitants. We could also track the arrival of the supply boats delivering food, letters and newspapers.

"So many dreams, hard work and plans," O'Laughlen said from the shadows under the window that first evening. "All come to naught."

Arnold nodded in hopeless assent. "Whatever the future may hold for us, this unforeseen turn of events will put us on terrain we never imagined."

As a doctor, I wondered what I might do to help my cellmates, but keeping my own spirits up quickly became a constant preoccupation.

That night, I lay on the wooden plank that served as a bed and for the first of countless nights entertained thoughts of escape and being with my family before offering this prayer: *Oh Lord, give me the strength to endure my time away from my loved ones, and get me released and home as soon as possible.*

I also sent prayers to my wife. *Dearest Frank, how I miss you. I cannot believe I am imprisoned here while you and our dear children are so far away. Please tell them that I will be home shortly, and know, my darling, just how much I love you all. Every day and every night I think about you and pray for you and Andrew, Lillian, Thomas and Sammy. Can you feel it? Do you know I will do anything to return to you?*

Praying about Frank brought back memories of our many years together. Sarah Frances Dyer—dubbed "Frank" from our teenage years because I had a sister named Sarah—had been my childhood sweetheart and the most beautiful and kind young lady I ever knew. She still is. She promised me she would wait for me until I completed my medical studies. She did just that, and we were married on Thanksgiving Day: November 26, 1857.

My father's wedding gift to us was "St. Catherine" Plantation, with 218 acres, a small road and 13 perches of land. It was originally part of the Oak Hill Plantation, established by my great-great-grandfather Thomas Mudd when he came to America in the 1640s.

Our home needed restoration before we could move in. Frank took on the project with such great enthusiasm that my respect for her and optimism for our future grew each day. It was a tobacco farm that required slaves to work the fields.

To avoid becoming slave owners, Frank and I "borrowed" workers from my father who lived nearby. Earlier this year I purchased a cook stove so Frank could cook indoors, and we added two new rooms for our children and patients who required longer-term care.

Every day since our imprisonment I have written Frank a letter, but do not know if or when she will receive them. Nor can I predict when I will hear from her, my parents, or George. I already find myself struggling to keep my faith during this ordeal, so I try not to think about my family except just before I fall sleep, which I have found brings me some comfort.

At least this cell is more comfortable than the ship's bilge. We could only climb topside for our rations of fat salt pork and hard biscuits, then had to return to our stifling and damp sleeping quarters, which stank of rotten vegetables and other ship supplies. On the final days of our voyage, our commander Captain George W. Dutton experienced a change of heart and allowed us to sleep on the deck cooled by ocean breezes. He ordered that our chains be removed during daylight hours.

When Ponce de Leon discovered these seven little islands in 1513, he was inspired by their population of large sea turtles, and christened the island *Las Tortugas*. A few years later the English re-named them *The Dry Tortugas* because they lacked natural water. Rain water is now collected from the roofs of the Fort and the surrounding buildings, but there is never enough. Supply boats occasionally bring fresh water; otherwise, we can only drink bad coffee.

The prisoner diet consists of bread, coffee, potatoes and onions. Yesterday they brought us some sort of rancid meat, which none of us tasted after smelling it. In addition to flour, the bread features bugs, sticks and dirt; we eat it anyway. My stomach is always growling and I constantly feel empty.

6

April 23, 1865

Booth and Herold disappeared into Zekiah Swamp after leaving Dr. Mudd's farm, slipping through the dense stands of old-growth hardwoods and marshland undergrowth. They set up a rudimentary camp in a frame of pines one quarter mile off the main road. Booth had left the boot from his injured leg at Dr. Mudd's house, so his foot and ankle were aching fiercely with cold and pain. Despite shivering almost uncontrollably in the damp swampy air, they couldn't risk attracting attention with a fire.

"Damn wind," muttered Herold, clutching his revolver close. "Look up at the pines thrashing to and fro."

Booth didn't answer as he struggled to curl himself into a comfortable position.

Stiff and hungry, they resumed their escape ride early the next morning, seeing no one until they reached the home of Samuel Cox, a middle-aged planter whose son had fought in the Confederate Army. Cox's home was about seven miles beyond Bryantown, and they arrived exhausted and irritable. He spurned the reward money offered for their capture and helped the men rest and fortify themselves until Thursday, April 20th.

Cox told them that posters urging citizens to turn in the fugitives had been distributed around the area. "You do know, my friends," he teased, "that they're offering a sizable reward for you."

"Really, and how much are we worth?" asked Booth, fascinated by the news.

"100,000 dollars!"

Herold's eyes grew wide, but Booth sneered. "That's all? Not nearly enough, is it? We'll never be famous with such a paltry amount."

"And I shall never be rich, hiding you in the thicket on my grounds," countered Cox.

"Then let us be on our way," snapped Booth. "Our lives are in danger."

Cox shook his head. "No, it is not safe to depart now. You must be prepared to hunker down in the woods until the coast is clear. I heard hoof beats earlier today—the Union Calvary is too close for comfort."

Booth grudgingly agreed. "You are in charge," he said quietly, almost sadly.

Cox kept the two hidden in the woods, sending his cousin Thomas A. Jones to provide them with food, brandy and newspapers. Before and after each delivery, Jones rode through the vicinity searching for patrol soldiers or scouts and listened to the sounds of the Calvary combing the countryside and woods.

"Shoot the horses lest their whinnying give you away," Jones advised them after his second visit. Herold led them down the road and into the dense woods and did as he was told.

They waited, wet and anxious. Booth turned his attention

to the newspapers, sharing the articles with his friend. He became enraged when he read that his actions were not being applauded.

"Look here," he ranted. "They are calling me the war's ultimate villain and saying that because of my actions, any kindly feeling toward the South has disappeared."

Herold grabbed the paper from him to read the article. "Hell, they say the killing is the most deplorable calamity ever to have befallen the people of the United States."

"And here in the *National Intelligencer*, they are lauding Lincoln as a true American hero. This is the paper I sent my letter to explaining my actions, and they never even printed it!" Booth's voice trembled with fury.

Then he took out his diary and chronicled his regrets, misunderstandings, hopes and desires. He carefully detailed his reasons for killing Lincoln so his point of view would be properly recorded for posterity.

I struck boldly and not as the papers say. I walked with a firm step through a thousand of his friends, was stopped, but pushed on. I can never repent it, though we hated to kill. Our country owed all her troubles to him, and God simply made men the instrument of his punishment.

Explaining himself this way seemed to help Booth get through the tedious and stressful days of waiting.

On the fifth day, Jones arrived with warm food and announced, "It's clear now. Are you strong enough to take a boat over the Potomac this evening?"

Booth nodded. He knew several of Cox's former slaves had seen him ride up, and wasn't certain they could be trusted to keep quiet.

Although still in considerable pain, Booth mounted a

borrowed horse and held precariously to its thick mane so he wouldn't fall off. He and Herold followed Jones to a small inlet where the boat was concealed. Shivering with cold and fever, he begged for coffee. "I need some deliverance from this Hell."

"It's too dangerous to light a fire," Jones told him. "Eat this cold meat and bread."

They pressed on. The steep descent down to the water was extremely arduous for John Wilkes Booth, but he knew it was his only chance. He allowed Herold and Jones to carry him the last few yards. Their 12-foot flat-bottomed boat had been tied to a large oak tree at the water's edge. Through the cold mist hovering over the surface of the wide Potomac, they could see Virginia on the other river bank and were encouraged that safety was finally in sight.

They also knew that they would have to navigate rough river currents and tides for just over two miles without being spotted by Union warship patrols. Before they shoved off, Jones gave them a final warning.

"There will be patrols out there hunting for two men in a small boat. It is common naval practice for ships to douse their running lights at night to thwart smugglers; be vigilant or you will run headlong into one of them."

Jones handed Booth a small candle to illuminate a compass pointed toward the southwest. "Keep going in that direction," he advised, and you will reach Machodoc Creek and the home of Mrs. Quesenberry. Just tell her you come from me, and she will take good care of you."

The fugitives thanked Jones. He returned home, his work completed.

Herold and Booth paddled hard for the opposite shore, with Herold doing most of the paddling. After several hours, Herold nudged Booth.

"Duck!" he called out. "Do you see the Navy patrol vessel ahead?"

It was too late. Shots rang out from behind the searchlights.

"Paddle for shore!" Herold shouted over the noise. "Keep your head low, and paddle like hell."

After a short time, they realized the Federal gunboat was no longer pursuing them.

"I think they let us go," whispered Booth. "Davy, do you think we are paddling in the wrong direction?"

It had become too dark to be certain. Eventually they reached land, just four miles from where they'd pushed off and still in Maryland. They were forced to hide their boat in the brush for another day, shivering under damp wool blankets.

After another twenty-four hours of hiding, sleeping and devouring the food Jones had left them, they set out again under the cover of darkness and rowed hard for Virginia. This time they made it. It was April 23rd.

And safety was still a long way off.

7

April 26, 1865

Lafayette Baker, the self-proclaimed "Chief of Union Intelligence," believed Booth would head for the Kentucky Mountains. That meant Booth would cross the river into Virginia. So he sent twenty-five members of the Sixteenth New York Cavalry by steamship to the wartime infantry base in Belle Plain, Virginia. They were commanded by his cousin Lieutenant Luther Baker.

The soldiers hurriedly deployed from Belle Plain and began canvassing the countryside, banging on farmhouse doors and questioning the occupants. They also stopped riders and carriages, pressing the travelers for information.

But nobody remembered seeing Booth or Herold. The Cavalry's steamboat was ready to return empty-handed back up the Rappahannock to Washington City from Port Royal. But when they showed the photographs one last time, two men on the dock positively identified their prey.

The extremely exhausted soldiers climbed back into their saddles and set off for more hours of riding.

The fugitives could sense their danger but were unaware of how close the soldiers were.

"Jones gave us the name of a guide to contact," Herold

reminded Booth. They found him quickly, and he secured a horse for Booth to ride.

The guide led them to the home of Dr. Richard Stuart, who would not operate on Booth's leg or even put them up overnight. He fed them a cold supper after Booth told him he was a former soldier injured at Petersburg and on his way home.

"We must continue," urged the guide. "Can you go further, John?"

Booth nodded. "I feel weary but I will try."

Several hours later, they found lodging in the shanty of a free black man named William Lucas. Their guide left them there.

The next morning Lucas hitched up a team and drove them inland to Port Conway, so they could catch the ferry across the Rappahannock River to Port Royal. While waiting for the ferry, they met three former Confederate soldiers on their way home.

Herold approached them and eventually determined their loyalties to the Confederacy.

"How do you feel about the war now that it is over?" Herold asked them.

"It is still a noble cause and we applaud the patriot who shot Lincoln," one of them replied vehemently. His companions nodded in assent.

When Herold pointed to Booth and confided that his companion was that patriot, they acted impressed and deferential.

"What can we do to help you, my friend?" they asked him.

"We need shelter so Booth can heal," answered Herold.

"Follow us," they answered, as they led him to the farm of a man named Richard Garrett, whose son had recently returned from the war.

Garrett resisted offering shelter until he was told that Booth was a wounded war veteran. He agreed to let them spend the night in their barn if the soldiers would return for them the following day. But he and his brother cautiously slept outside the barn in case the men planned to steal their horses and escape.

The following afternoon, Union soldiers in Bowling Green, Virginia, heard about two suspicious men from one of the three Confederates. Once the Rebel soldier understood the danger he was in, he chose to save himself by telling them where Booth and Herold were hiding.

On April 26, at about 1:00 a.m., a mounted patrol swung in through the gate and demanded entry into the house. Booth and Herold were sleeping in the tobacco barn.

The soldiers surrounded the barn and ordered them to come out.

"You must surrender now, or we will light up the barn," demanded Lieutenant Baker.

"Booth, we must go," urged Herold. "We will be burned to death if we don't."

Booth considered his options. He would likely die either way, and he knew it.

After spending so much time with the man on the run, Booth watched in amazement as Herold begged and pleaded in the most piteous manner to surrender.

"Go, Davy. I will take my chances," he responded, shaking his head in disgust. "You are a damned coward for surrendering."

Booth called out in a clear, melodious voice. "Captain, there is a man here who wishes to surrender."

"Bring out the arms and you can come," shouted Lieutenant Baker.

Booth called out, "He has no arms; they are mine, and I shall keep them."

Herold was ordered to extend his hands through the doors, which he did, as an officer pulled him out and closed the door.

Again Lieutenant Baker called out, "We have fifty men armed with carbines and pistols around the barn. You cannot escape."

Booth considered this, and answered. "Captain, this is a hard case. Give a lame man a chance. Draw up your men twenty yards from the door, and I will fight your whole command."

"We did not come to fight, but to take you. We've got you, so you had best surrender."

Booth replied. "Give me a little time to consider."

Baker said, "Very well, take your time. You can have five minutes."

With his flair for the dramatic, John Wilkes Booth took his full five minutes. He then approached the door before making his final argument.

"Captain, I believe you are an honorable and brave man. I have had a half dozen opportunities to shoot you, and have a bead drawn on you now, but do not wish to do it. Withdraw your forces a hundred yards from the door and I will come out. Give me a chance for my life, for I will not be taken alive."

Baker had tired of the game. "We have waited long enough. Come out now or we will fire the barn."

Booth answered in his peculiar stage cadence. "Well, my brave boys, then prepare a stretcher for me."

Colonel Granger stepped forward and lit a match to some hay. Flames crackled through timbers and hay as Booth began to smell the sickly sweet wood smoke of burning cedar. He looked across the barn just as Lieutenant Baker opened the door.

The door was opened in order to give Booth a chance to come out in full view. They could see him leaning against a haymow supported by his crutch, with a carbine in one hand and a pistol in the other. Turning toward them on his crutch, he straightened up to his full height and dramatically prepared to begin his final scene like a cornered wild beast.

A cloud of smoke rolled to the roof, sweeping across the room. Booth looked to be standing in an arch of fire and smoke for an instant, then dropped his crutch and dashed for the door, carbine and pistol in his hands. Gasping for air and staggering, he tried to shout out. He heard the crack of a pistol and felt a sharp jolt in his neck. Booth reeled forward, throwing up one hand, and fell face downward on the hay scattered on the floor.

Lieutenant Baker ran in, followed by Conger, Doherty and young Garrett. Officer Baker seized him by the arms, intending to secure him in case he had only been stunned. When he turned him over, a pistol was found in his hand, still held with a vise-like grip.

It was later discovered that Sergeant Boston Corbett

had fired the shot from a navy revolver through a crevice in the rear of the barn. The ball struck Booth on the side of the neck, a little back of center, and passed entirely through, breaking the spinal cord.

Nothing more was heard from inside the barn.

Baker and Conger rushed into the flames to drag Booth outside. They laid him under a tree, and offered him water.

The actor was alive, but barely. "No, thank you," he wheezed hoarsely. "I ask only that you tell my mother that I died for my country."

The bullet had sliced through Booth's spinal cord and paralyzed him. The decision was made not to transport him, but to make him as comfortable as possible. He died before morning, and his limp body was laid in the back of a garbage wagon.

John Wilkes Booth's life had come to an end. He was twenty-six years old.

8

APRIL 24, 1865

April 24, 1865 will always symbolize the end of my freedom. Because of my earlier interrogations with Lovett and Wells, and my two signed statements, I was taken into custody that day and briefly imprisoned in Washington City's Old Capitol Prison—Carroll Annex.

It all happened so quickly. On April 21st, following the second interview with the detectives at my farm, Lovett took me into custody and delivered me to Colonel H. H. Wells in Bryantown, who was in command of the soldiers quartered there. While we rode to Bryantown, I made the ill-fated decision to tell Lovett I had made the acquaintance of John Wilkes Booth the previous year.

It is hard to explain why I brought the unfortunate subject up; perhaps because during my years in medical practice I tried to be as helpful and forthcoming as possible. Or, maybe I forgot that Lovett had very different goals than I—and was in a position to do my family and me excessive harm.

"Sir, I want you to know that I was introduced to John Wilkes Booth sometime in November of last year."

Lovett pivoted sharply in the saddle. "By whom?" he barked.

"John Thompson. We were attending Sunday services at St. Mary's Church in Bryantown."

"And Booth just happened to be there?" asked Lovett, sarcastically. "Or, were you meeting there with members of the Confederate underground?"

I winced, because I had attended several of those meetings, but not when Booth was present.

"No, Sir. He was introduced to me because he wanted to inspect my farm. Thompson told him I might be interested in selling it."

"Then what happened?"

"I showed him the farm and he seemed to like it. Then he asked me to help him find a horse, and we went to George Gardiner's house, since I knew he had a one-eyed horse he was willing to sell."

"Did he buy it?" he asked.

"Yes, he bought the horse." I paused, waiting for the next question. When it did not follow, I explained that Booth never made an offer on the farm.

"How long did he stay?"

I cleared my throat, recognizing the magnitude of my mistake and trying to be careful. "It was dark by then, so I invited him to stay the night. We went over to Gardiner's place early the next morning."

We arrived in Bryantown. I was handed a photograph portrait of Booth and asked if it resembled the man I knew. I told them it was not a clear likeness of the injured stranger. I wasn't able to see his face while treating him as it was covered with a shawl and turned away from me.

I felt terrified when they told me to write a statement summarizing what I had related during interrogation,

since they were so intent on finding discrepancies or con-
flicts. It turned out they were most interested in this rec-
ollection:

*I first heard of the assassination of President Lincoln on
Saturday afternoon about two or three o'clock in the
afternoon.*

Colonel Wells reminded me that during an earlier interrogation, I had mentioned hearing of the assassination
during the church service that Sunday. It seemed to annoy
him that I had two versions of the story, but they finally
allowed me to go back to the farm with instructions to
return the next morning to answer more questions.

When I arrived, Wells had prepared a statement for
me to read and sign. They wanted a better description of
the injured man, so I added more details to the description given the day before.

*He was a man, I should suppose about five feet ten
inches high, and appeared to be pretty well made, but
had a heavy shawl on all the time. His hair was black
and seemed to be somewhat inclined to curl; it was worn
long. He had a pretty full forehead and his skin was fair.
He was very pale when I saw him, and appeared as if
accustomed to in-door rather than out-door life. I have
been shown the photograph of J. Wilkes Booth and I
should not think that this was the man from any resemblance to the photograph, but from other causes I have
every reason to believe that he is the man whose leg I
dressed as previously stated.*

I also acknowledged, for the first time in writing, the prior meeting with Booth. This admission would soon seal my doom.

And my next signed statement proved to be even more disastrous.

I have never seen Booth since that time to my knowledge until last Saturday night.

I went home, knowing that I had not convinced them of my innocence. Colonel Wells had ordered that I be taken into custody on Monday, April 24th, and transported to Washington City, where I was imprisoned in the Old Capitol Prison (Carroll Annex). My personal nightmare had begun.

"You will be held as a witness, not a suspect." Those were Colonel Well's final words to me. He failed to mention that the group the government identified as Booth's co-conspirators—Samuel Arnold, Michael O'Laughlen, Mary Surratt, Lewis Powell, George Atzerodt, Dave Herold and Edman Spangler—would be held at Washington's Arsenal Penitentiary. And that I would be joining them at the trial.

I later learned that the day I arrived in Washington City, anxious and uncertain of my fate, John Wilkes Booth was at the farmhouse of Richard Garrett near Port Royal, Virginia, with just one more day to live.

9

At the onset of the Civil War, the government converted the aging red-brick Hill's Boarding House into a jail, renaming it the Old Capitol Prison. Its windows, overlooking the broad Capitol lawn, were fitted with bars. Its rotting vermin and rat-infested walls provided scant protection from icy winter winds.

The cell I shared with several other prisoners reeked of decay and measured a scarce ten-by-twelve feet. One prisoner referred to the prison as "the gloomiest, most terrible-looking prison in the land." The food served was greasy, moldy, mushy and barely half-cooked. Dust and cobwebs covered everything in the cells, which were jammed to overflowing. Two soldiers left me there on April 24th, after my interrogation in Maryland.

My cell in a wooden annex known as Carroll Annex was just like the rooms in the main prison. Both were overpopulated and filthy; our food was simply dreadful. Yet I remained determined to hold on to my sanity, believing that a positive attitude was the only choice I had to survive my short time here.

On my fifth day in prison, I sat down and wrote a letter to my wife.

Dearest Frank, I am well. Hope you and the children are enjoying a like blessing. Try and get someone to plant our crop. It is very uncertain what time I shall be released from here. Hire hands at the prices they demand. Urge them on all you can and make them work. I am truly in hopes my stay here will be short, and know not when I can return again to your fond embrace and to our little children.

I had no idea of how extensive the dragnet had become as it raced with a vengeance across the country. Rounding up Lincoln's killers had become a national obsession. Secretary of War Stanton was charged with identifying the larger conspiracy that exploded from Booth's single gunshot. The idiosyncratic Lafayette Baker was pushed out of the limelight when Secretary Stanton took control.

I eventually learned a little about some of the other prisoners, several of whom came from southern Maryland. The Virginia doctor who had given Booth a free meal was included, as were the livery stable operator who rented Booth his horse, a Portuguese sea captain, and even the owner of Ford's Theatre—although he had been a hundred miles away the night of President Lincoln's assassination.

Some prisoners considered too important to be incarcerated with us at Carroll or at the Old Capitol were being held aboard two Union warships anchored in the Anacostia River.

Sometime later, I put together the bits and pieces of information about Booth's murder plot, which had begun as a kidnapping plot and was definitely not a one-man operation. One man was assigned to hold Booth's horse. Two others were scheduled to kill the Secretary of State. Yet another was supposed to shoot or stab the Vice President, while two more were to stand by and provide assistance where needed. And finally, there remained one unfortunate woman—the owner of the house where most of the conspiracy was organized.

By the time I reached my cell, six members of the ring had been taken into custody; of that group, only two of us were not held on a ship—the woman, Mary Surratt, and myself. Mary's son, John H. Surratt Jr., was suspected of being a part of the conspiracy, but was still at large. He seemed to have escaped and eluded justice.

Each of us had a slightly different version on the kidnapping plan; I can only speak of my direct involvement. I was cognizant of and had agreed to Booth's original plan in August 1864, which involved capturing President Lincoln and exchanging him for Confederate prisoners needed to replenish the Confederate Army's ranks. For the next eight months Booth took no overt action to carry out this strategy, so I believed the plot had been abandoned. When he eventually called the kidnapping conspirators together again, I was not invited and did not attend.

On March 15, 1865, he gave his group his new outline in a Washington City restaurant. "We will handcuff Lincoln in his box at Ford's Theatre, lower him by rope from the box to the theater stage, and then carry him out of the theater to a waiting carriage," he explained to them.

"And then what?" asked Lewis Powell, visibly stunned by Booth's words.

"Then we shall flee the city with the captured Lincoln."

Sam Arnold stood up. "I agreed to capture the President in a country setting, but I vehemently disagree with this plan to do it at the theater!"

"Yes, John, it is most impractical, and also dangerous for all involved," argued George Atzerodt.

John Surratt had a different objection. "Besides, General Grant has since resumed prisoner exchanges, so why even carry out a kidnapping plan at this time?"

By the meeting's end everyone had voiced opposition to Booth's revised plan. So two days later, when he heard that the President would be attending a play at Campbell Hospital—a "country setting"—Booth hurriedly assembled the conspirators once more. At the last minute, President Lincoln had a change of plans and never visited the hospital. Sam Arnold and Michael O'Laughlen concluded that the idea of kidnapping Lincoln was a bad one. They dropped out of the group and returned to Baltimore.

One month later President Lincoln was assassinated. Detectives tracked down Sam Arnold through a letter he wrote to Booth, and arrested him at his new job at Fortress Monroe. Arnold then implicated Michael O'Laughlen, who would be arrested at his sister's house in Baltimore.

* * *

As part of trial preparations, we were all taken to the old Arsenal building, located on a peninsula called Greenleaf's Point. We were thrown into a series of damp, narrow warrens, and except for Mary Surratt, were all shackled and hooded.

"Hooding" prisoners is a vicious form of torture. Canvas bags without eye openings and very tiny slits for our noses and mouths were pulled over our heads. We were forced to breathe and feed ourselves through these small slits. Cotton padding was pressed against the eyes and ears; during hot summer days, our faces would swell and itch intolerably. As a doctor, I tried to explain that this torture might cause panic attacks or even worse, but my objections were ignored. Eventually one man was driven insane by the brutal constraints.

10

Sometimes you run your life backwards in your mind to see at what point you might have made things turn out differently. It is quite difficult to accept the fact that we can only affect the future, no matter how much you would like to revisit and change your past. I know I will always reflect on what occurred and wonder: *was this where I could have stopped my life from going down this path?*

In hindsight, I could recognize several critical mistakes. I did not know the extent of damning evidence the government had collected when it presented its case against me. They knew about Booth and Herold's visit when I treated Booth's injury. They knew I was a former slaveholder and a Southern sympathizer who had opposed Lincoln's administration. And they knew, thanks to my guileless admission, that I had met Booth in November of 1864.

It turned out they were also aware of my second meeting with John H. Surratt, Jr. That encounter in December of 1864 in Washington City seriously undermined my claim of innocence. It was revealed by one of the government's star witnesses in my trial, Louis J. Weichmann.

My own reckless words further damaged my case. After telling Colonel Wells I met with Booth in November,

1864, I asserted, "I have never seen Booth since that time to my knowledge until last Saturday night (April 15th)." What a fool I was. How misguided was this attempt to protect my family from more hardship; yet that is no excuse for my stupid lie.

And that wasn't my final lie of the day. I had not taken Booth to George Gardiner's house to buy his horse during his visit in November as I said; Booth had not spent the night in my home then either. He stayed the night and purchased his horse during our third meeting. I hid this meeting from Wells in another attempt to hinder the prosecution for my family's sake. Here is what actually occurred:

On December 18th, following the service at St. Mary's Church, Booth and I again met at the Bryantown Tavern. I had arranged a meeting with Thomas Harbin, a Confederate Secret Service operative who worked in several undercover operations in the lower Maryland counties bordering the Potomac River. Booth wanted him to help transport the captured Lincoln to Richmond.

Afterwards, Booth returned to my home and spent the night. On December 19th, Thomas Gardiner sold the one-eyed horse to Booth. Two witnesses testified to seeing him at St. Mary's Church near Bryantown on two separate occasions.

The same misguided desire to be forthright finally damaged my legal state irretrievably. During the journey to Fort Jefferson in the Dry Tortugas my military guard was commanded by Captain George W. Dutton, of Company C, 10th Regiment, Veteran Reserve Corps. I confided to Captain Dutton that I *might* have recognized the man being treated in my home after learning that President

Lincoln had been shot. I also explained that he wore a disguise which confused both my wife and me. I told him his face was covered almost entirely by a shawl. I agreed to having been with Booth at the National Hotel on the evening referred to by witness Louis J. Weichmann, and that I went to Washington on that occasion to meet Booth by appointment concerning an introduction to John Surratt.

Captain Dutton wrote an affidavit concerning my conversational statements and filed it with Brigadier General Joseph Holt, the Judge Advocate General, on July 22, 1865. That was the most damaging claim to date. I am ashamed and saddened that I felt I could trust the captain with my confession. What a reckless, idiotic mistake.

Now I must prepare an affidavit to respond to Captain Dutton's claims. I will admit to the meeting at the National Hotel and introducing Booth to John Surratt Jr. I will mention Booth's initial offer to purchase my land, to which I agreed. I will not confess to having recognized Booth while attending to his injury.

On April 15, 1865, I responded as any good doctor would when faced with a stranger in desperate need of medical assistance—my Hippocratic Oath required it of me. Later, finally suspicious of my two late night guests, I voluntarily informed the military authorities of their visit.

More importantly, I will include in my affidavit that I am bewildered and disappointed that for the innocent acts stated above, I was taken into custody and eventually charged as an accomplice in the murder of the President, and in aiding and abetting John Wilkes Booth's attempt to escape.

11

MAY 12, 1865

On May 1st, President Johnson convened a Military Commission to try us as "conspirators" in the assassination of President Lincoln. The Commanding Officer overseeing the trial would be Major General Winfield Scott Hancock.

On the morning of May 9th, the guards escorted us to a courtroom on the top floor of the Arsenal. Our hoods were removed and we were led stumbling, trembling and blinking into the brightness of the day, and then up the stairs to the courtroom. I struggled to maintain some dignity, knowing how dirty and disheveled we appeared. I tried to calm myself, despite the stunning realization that something was now happening that couldn't possibly be happening to me. The fact that I was being charged with *conspiring to murder President Abraham Lincoln* was an inconceivable nightmare coming true.

I was surrounded by a crowd of grim-faced senior military officers, some high-ranking civilians, reporters, judges and guards.

I knew my wife Frank had already contracted a lawyer. My support was led by General Thomas Ewing, a thirty-year-old General in the Union Army and a former

Chief Justice of the Kansas Supreme Court. Ewing also happened to be the brother-in-law of one of the Union's top war heroes—General William T. Sherman. I found what comfort I could in the General's excellent credentials, and trusted he would mount a strong defense for me and two other accused conspirators—Ned Spangler and Sam Arnold. He would be assisted by Counsel Frederick Stone.

Mary Surratt was represented by Reverdy Johnson, a former Maryland Senator and a U.S. Attorney General, as well as F.A. Aiken and John W. Clampitt.

Our prospects were decidedly grim. The country was out for blood and wanted a speedy closure of this heinous chapter in American history. Members of the Court would feel the pressure of millions of citizens expecting a prompt execution of justice. I could see the weight of this pressure in the faces of the military judges scowling at the group of defendants.

Major Generals David Hunter and Lew Wallace headed up the Court, and I shuddered with foreboding sitting in front of them. Major General Hunter, a long-time friend of President Lincoln, was expected to deal harshly with anyone identified as a conspirator. My attorney had already voiced displeasure and concern because the trial was to be held before a military tribunal. He objected vigorously when he learned my case would be judged under "the common law of war," when no such law even existed.

The government's Chief Counsel, Joseph Holt, had been United States Army Judge Advocate General. He was proud of his reputation as an extremely tough prosecutor, and we were warned he would push for conviction. He was also adamantly opposed to anything related to the Confederacy, slavery, or secession—everything we stood for. Let me be honest: I had fully supported the Confederate cause and at times volunteered to help move Confederate mail through routes in southern Maryland. These facts would later be held against me in the trial.

I looked around at the other prisoners, whose lives and freedom would be judged along with mine. Some of them I knew; others I knew not. My opinions about their defense statements would be tested.

Lewis Powell, alias Lewis Payne, a twenty-year-old giant of a man, had been given an important role by Booth on the night of the assassination. He cajoled his way into the home of Secretary of State William H. Seward intending to stab him to death. But Seward was wearing a brace from an earlier accident and the knife failed to find the target. Lewis's mental state had drifted slowly into madness after being forced to wear the canvas hood.

David Herold was a twenty-three-year-old pharmacist's clerk with a stooped figure. His naiveté befitted a man much younger than he. He had accompanied Powell to Seward's home and held the horse's reins to effect a quick escape, yet ran away when a servant rushed outside screaming for help.

He had been in my home while I treated Booth, and I recognized him immediately. David accompanied Booth during the entire twelve-day escape attempt, from the night of the assassination until he was captured at the Garrett farm.

George A. Atzerodt was a thirty-three-year-old carriage

maker and blockade runner, with a sickly nature, a consumptive cough and a "villainous" appearance. Booth had chosen him to kill Vice President Andrew Johnson at the same time that Lincoln and Seward were being assassinated. Losing his nerve, he spent the night getting drunk in a tavern instead. He did not learn about the assassination until the next day.

Edman (Ned) Spangler was forty years old and a stagehand at Ford's Theatre. His life had been frugal and simple—sleeping at Ford's Theatre and taking his meals at a nearby boardinghouse. I would later discover he was an expert carpenter who had worked at the Booth family estate in Bel Air, Maryland. He was supposed to hold Booth's horse during the theater production, but had been too busy working and asked an assistant to tend to the horse instead. Spangler's only service was to block one man who was chasing Booth. Several observers mistakenly thought Spangler had helped Booth flee from the theater and reported this to the authorities, who arrested him as a co-conspirator. His boss, John T. Ford, considered him a valuable employee without any role in the assassination.

Samuel Arnold was a twenty-eight-year-old former Confederate soldier and Booth's school mate. His father owned one of Baltimore's largest bakeries. When the Civil War broke out, he and his two brothers joined the Confederate Army. He was discharged for medical reasons and worked for a time in Georgia, returning to Baltimore in 1864. He participated in both unsuccessful presidential kidnap attempts before washing his hands of the plot and moving away. Although he had known nothing about the assassination and had been in Baltimore when it happened, Arnold was still indicted and stood trial.

Michael O'Laughlen, aka *O'Laughlin* was twenty-seven years old and like Arnold, a former Confederate soldier from Baltimore and a boyhood friend of Booth. He worked in the family hay and feed business. Also like Arnold, he knew about the kidnapping plan but had refused to be a participant in a murder. He had been on a drinking spree at several different Washington taverns the night of the shooting. And now he would also be fighting for his life.

Mrs. Mary E. Surratt was a forty-five-year-old widow with a sweet smile and a buxom figure. I met Mary once before, but did not know her. Her son John Surratt was a Confederate agent from Maryland who had also participated in the kidnapping attempts, but refused to have anything to do with an assassination. Mary owned the boardinghouse where the plotters gathered on several occasions. She also agreed to conceal weapons and other items for Booth to use during his escape.

Reflecting on our group of defendants, I sincerely believed that Mary and I were innocent of any crime. We had not been part of the kidnapping plot, nor had we participated in (or known about) the assassination plans.

The trial of the century was about to begin. On May 12, 1865, the first witness was sworn in. Nearly three hundred and fifty witnesses would testify over the next six weeks. It would be four days before the government finally called the first witness against me.

And I was ready to tell the truth.

12

JUNE 12, 1865

I chose not to panic or break down under the pressure of my interrogation. I wanted to believe that justice would prevail and that everything would work out for me once the judges realized what an appalling mistake the charges against me were.

My attorney, General Ewing, had found me clothing that almost fit my slender frame.

Smiling, he joked about my image. "Sam, with those mild blue eyes and dark auburn hair, you will appear more credible in this outfit. Just keep your hopeful and confident air about you."

But as the questions continued day after day, I started believing that the Court was trying to make me *appear guilty.* Two witnesses hinted that I had not fully cooperated with the authorities. True, I had not immediately mentioned Booth's visit to authorities out of concern for my family; but my intent had never been to give Booth more of a head start in his escape journey.

"That is untrue, Sir," I calmly responded, refuting this falsehood.

"And you claimed you did not recognize the fugitive's

photograph when it was shown to you," prodded the prosecutor. "Is that correct?"

I sat quietly, my pressed shirtsleeves rolled up, a damp cloth knotted around my neck. "It did not resemble him, so at first I was unsure," I said. "Later, I agreed that it could be."

The courtroom was only thirty feet long and twenty-five feet wide, and seemed to be overrun with people. The judges sat at one covered table, while the prosecutors and defense counsel crowded around another. The rest of the packed space was taken up by reporters and spectators. The air inside the room was stale and still. Hot air rolled over us as if we were sitting before a hot oven.

The other prisoners were seated behind a railed-off section; Mary Surratt and I, having been the last to be brought in, were outside the railing. After complaints of "preferential treatment" were instigated by several defending attorneys, and even a written letter of complaint to Major General Hancock, this objection was overruled.

We defendants understood that our lives were on the line. We all heard the speculation, rumors and gossip surrounding our cases, followed occasionally by table pounding and loud arguments.

I watched and listened as two dozen witnesses testified against me. I didn't think any of their testimonies were damaging. They needed to establish that I knew who Booth and Herold were when they came to my farm (*harboring fugitives*) and that I knew what had been done (*an accessory after the fact*). I didn't believe they were successful in proving either one.

They also had to demonstrate beyond a reasonable doubt that I had been a part of the conspiracy itself, and had known about the plot to kill the President. My attorney explained that the first of these goals was impossible to prove. Only four persons could testify as to whether I recognized my visitors: Booth was dead, Herold was not allowed to testify, and my wife and I swore upon the Bible that we hadn't recognized the man with the beard and muffler as the actor John Wilkes Booth. Neither Frank nor I had ever seen Herold before his visit to our farm.

Regarding the second accusation, the government's case hinged on sworn testimony given by four men. The most damaging came from Louis Weichmann, one of Mrs. Surratt's boarders. He recalled having met Booth and me several months earlier in Washington City.

"John Surratt and I were walking down Seventh Street in Washington. We met Mudd and Booth and went to Booth's room in the National Hotel for drinks and cigars."

"What happened after that?"

"Well, the others went into the hallway for a private chat, while Booth scribbled a map on the back of an envelope."

"Did you know where the map led?" General Ewing asked him.

"Uh huh, because Booth wanted to buy Dr. Mudd's farm property, so I reckon it was the trail to his place."

"And did you hear anything in the hotel room indicating that Booth, Surratt and Dr. Mudd were involved in a conspiracy of some kind?"

"No, Sir, I did not."

"How were you able to remember the date of the meeting in mid-January?"

"It was after Christmas vacation, and I just got a letter dated January 6th, so it had to be around mid-month."

"Did you ever see Dr. Mudd at the boardinghouse?" asked my attorney.

"No, Sir, I never did."

I heard this and said nothing. I knew the meeting had actually taken place on December 23rd, 1864. It is interesting to note that years later, in his autobiography, Weichmann said he and Surratt had been Christmas shopping.

The second government witness, William A. Evans, claimed he had a secret but unpaid commission to arrest "deserters and dis-loyalists."

"I saw Dr. Mudd last winter entering the Surratt House on H Street. It was a nest of spies. I saw Mrs. Surratt's daughter Anna greet him as she opened the door."

My eyes widened in surprise. I had never met Anna Surratt. In rebuttal, Anna was placed on the stand, and affirmed that she had never met me.

"I met Booth, Powell and Atzerodt in the boardinghouse, but never saw Dr. Mudd there," she testified.

Next on the stand was a New York attorney, Marcus Norton.

"What is your relationship to Dr. Mudd?"

He seemed to be taken aback by the question, as was I. I had no idea who this man was.

"On March 3rd, 1865, I was preparing some court papers in my room at the National Hotel. A stranger appeared at my door looking for John Wilkes Booth. I told him how to reach Booth's room."

"Do you recognize that man today?" asked the defense attorney.

He nodded. "Yes, Sir. He is there," he responded, pointing at me across the room.

I shook my head, sweat slicking my skin. I hoped my attorney would ask him how long he laid eyes on me. He did ask, and the answer was "less than a minute."

His false testimony was undermined when my attorney, General Ewing, produced four witnesses—including a patient staying in my house for treatment—proving that I had not been within thirty miles of Washington on March 3rd or any other day that week. In my favor, he also brought in two of Norton's neighbors, including a local judge, who testified that they never believed anything the attorney said, and "that was the general opinion of the people of the area."

The government's last witness was Daniel J. Thomas, who gave falsified information about a visit between me, him and another farmer named John Downing. He claimed I had predicted, during a conversation we had about the war, that the President, the Cabinet and others would be killed in approximately six or seven weeks.

My attorney put John Downing on the witness stand.

"You have heard the claim about the war conversation, Mr. Downing. Were you present during this exchange?"

"Yes, indeed I was."

"Did the conversation take place as reported?"

"No, Sir, not at all. I was privy to everything said. Dr. Mudd never mentioned anything about anyone being killed."

Two other character witnesses also helped cast doubt on Daniel Thomas's testimony: his brother, a medical doctor, testified that Daniel suffered from "nervous depression," which affected his memory and sense of reason.

Another doctor, who had examined Daniel Thomas, corroborated that he was a compulsive liar as well as mentally unbalanced.

Prosecutor Holt had no real evidence to present against me, so the two attorneys spent an inordinate amount of time battling over a simple effort to notify the Army about Booth's visit.

During his defense, General Ewing built up a picture of a kindly country doctor awakened in the middle of the night to treat a stranger's broken leg. He explained that Dr. Mudd's house was miles away from Booth's escape route, and that Booth only detoured there because of his pain. He verified that Booth had been to the farm once before and remembered the route, but did not want to be recognized by Dr. Mudd so he wore a disguise.

My attorney called more witnesses, who confirmed that I had gone into Bryantown on medical errands, where I learned about the assassination. He corroborated that upon my return to the farm I discussed the matter with Frank, and together we decided to ask my cousin George to notify the authorities.

Prosecutor Holt tried to depict me as a Southern sympathizer responsible for delaying the pursuit of Booth.

Attorney Ewing argued. "What do you say to the fact that government investigators waited more than twenty-four hours before acting on Dr. Mudd's crucial message?"

Holt realized that his entire case revolved around raising suspicions and doubts. He also tried to use the fact that slaves worked on my farm to degrade my character.

"So, you are a slave owner, Dr. Mudd?" he smirked.

I smiled slowly. "No, Sir. I cannot afford to own slaves.

The slaves who work for us come from the farms of my father and my brother-in-law."

At cross-examination, General Ewing called a few of the slaves to the stand.

"Tell us about Dr. Mudd's character and his treatment of you," he prodded.

"He be real good to us, an' he care fer us jes' like de whites," answered Jeb Walker.

"Do you mean he treated you in his home?" asked my attorney.

"Yes, Suh. When we took sick, he wuz our doctah. He wuz wif' Marshall's wife wen she be sick wif' de typhoid, and dat be fer 'bout twenty days.'"

General Ewing also brought in friends, neighbors, and relatives to testify that I was a kind and considerate man. He proved that I took my oath of loyalty "with respect and reverence," and that I had called President Lincoln's death "an atrocious and revolting crime."

In spite of his noble attempt, I grew increasingly dispirited and confused as to why my innocence wasn't evident to everyone.

Finally, on June 12th, General Ewing was ready to make his final summation to the Court.

"Dr. Mudd is a good, peaceable and quiet citizen. He has neither murdered anyone or been proven guilty of treason. He did not participate in any plots against the President, and did not even know the latter was dead when Booth arrived at his house. He made every effort possible to establish contact with the search parties."

He paused, tossing a quick smile in my direction. "Moreover, the doctor had saved the notorious boot for the inspection of the authorities. He gave them all the information about Booth's broken leg, the treatment, and the conversations he and Frank had with both men. He even told them which escape route the fugitives took through the swamp."

And his final words revived my vanishing hopes.

"I wish to remind you that no one had traced Booth to Dr. Mudd's house. Had it not been through information supplied voluntarily by Dr. Mudd himself, the search parties would never have learned of the visit."

We recessed, and I was returned to my cell. All I could do now was pray.

13

July 7, 1865

About noon on July 6th, 1865, Major Generals W.S. Hancock and J.F. Hartranft visited our cells to announce the court's findings, as approved by President Johnson. The official records of the trial contained no information about how each of the nine military judges voted. However, six or more of the military judges must have voted "Guilty" for David Herold, George Atzerodt, Lewis Powell, and Mary Surratt; in a military trial a two-thirds majority was required to pass the death penalty. These four were sentenced to death by hanging.

Mary Surratt's physical appearance had changed drastically since the trial began. Severe cramps, excessive menstrual bleeding and a constant need to urinate were the result of a disease called endometriosis. Unable to care for herself in her cell, she depended on her daughter. Anna fought tirelessly to gain access to her mother's cell and help attend to her hygiene.

After her death sentence was announced, Mary's priest and her attorney rushed to request an urgent personal audience with President Andrew Johnson. They felt if they could explain her innocence in person, he might be persuaded to grant her a pardon.

"Condemned to be hanged?" shouted her attorney Frederick Aiken upon hearing the verdict. "She was merely a single woman trying to make ends meet. She was nowhere near Ford's Theatre, and certainly did not pull the trigger!"

Throughout the night, Mary, Anna, and her supporters remained hopeful, praying to God to spare her life. Mary refused to eat breakfast, believing she would be granted an audience with the President. At dawn, Mary's attorney and her daughter visited the White House in a last-ditch attempt *to appeal to the heart and tender mercies of the President.*

Less than an hour later they were told: "The President will not be interviewed by anyone on behalf of the condemned. He will not see Miss Surratt."

Her priest, Father Jacob Walter, also made an attempt to gain the ear of the President, with the same results; and so the dreaded hour approached.

At 11:00 a.m., her visitors were sent away so preparations could be completed. She changed into a clean black dress and veil, then stood quietly as they gently bound her ankles and wrists.

"Anna, try to remain hopeful," she whispered to her daughter, pupils black and huge. "There is still time."

She was led out into the blazing summer sun.

All it would have taken to spare her was one word from President Johnson. Mary continued praying that the words of her priest and her attorney had touched the President's heart.

She moved her gaze slowly up the ten-foot-high gallows scaffolding, built overnight for the four executions. Then she looked down at the freshly dug graves beneath the gallows. With a shutter she continued praying. *Oh Lord, will my body lay here for all of eternity?*

She, Lewis Powell, George Atzerodt and David Herold were led slowly up the gallows' staircase by a priest or a pastor. Father Walter and Father Wigget of the Catholic Church supported Mary and presented crucifixes for her to kiss. Suddenly weakened, she was given a chair.

Powell, aka Payne, stood bold and defiant in his fitted sailor suit that set off his robust figure to good advantage. Herold seemed thoroughly dazed by the situation. Atzerodt quaked with fear.

Anna whimpered, crying out "Mama" as she stood there with one hundred civilians gathered to watch the hanging. Of all those present, there was not one individual in the crowd who did not believe or hold hope that a reprieve would come for Mary Surratt.

Their arms were tied to their sides; their legs were tied at the ankles and knees so they would not kick during their death throes.

An anguished cry ripped across the courtyard. "Mrs. Surratt is innocent! Spare her!" It was Lewis Powell, tears streaming down his cheeks just before a cotton hood was pulled over his head.

Mary remained hopeful; after speaking with her Lord for over twenty hours she was not ready to give up. Her lips continued moving as she closed her eyes.

Soldiers were stationed next to couriers with swift horses between the White House and the Arsenal, in case the President decided to extend a last-minute pardon.

The muggy air grew heavy with anticipation as the crowd inside the penitentiary held their collective breath.

Just one word from the President, she prayed. *Dear Lord, please spare me. I did no wrong.*

She turned to face her executioner. "Please don't let me fall. I have vertigo."

He wordlessly placed a white hood over her head. Now she stood completely alone, terrified of tumbling forward over the edge before the pardon could arrive. She stood very straight and took in as much oxygen as she could. Then she slowly exhaled.

The death sentences were read aloud in alphabetical order by General Winfield Scott Hancock as each trapdoor was being propped up by a single post. Underneath the scaffold, four hand-selected members of the armed forces steadied themselves to kick away the posts upon General Hartranft's signal.

No one approached. A loud wailing filled the yard. Mary remembered to forgive her son John for not rescuing her at the cost of his own life. She prayed to her Lord to give Anna strength to endure the painful days to come. Tears filled her eyes; her chest began heaving with fear.

The brittle shout "Pull!" seemed enveloped in the painful silence of the crowd, then punctuated by the sound of the pins being kicked loose. At 1:28 p.m., the trapdoors swung open and four bodies plummeted six feet in one second. Only Atzerodt attempted to say anything before the trap was sprung: "Gentlemen, take war—." His sentence was finished in eternity.

Because her body was lighter, Mary's neck did not break during her fall and she did not die instantly. She swayed for five interminable minutes before her larynx was crushed and her body no longer fought for air.

General Hartranft allowed the bodies to swing above the still-stunned crowd for twenty more minutes, then had them cut down and carried into the building to be prepared for burial. The judges congratulated themselves on a job well done and moved on to other assignments.

Mary Surratt became the first and only woman hanged by the United States government during the Civil War period.

14

July 17, 1865

On July 6th we were seated in our cell and wondering what our futures had in store. Major Generals W.S. Hancock and J.F. Hartranft unlocked the bolt on the door and walked in. I didn't care for their grim expressions as Hancock handed us copies of a document.

"Here is the order for your sentences," Hancock told us, without preamble. "It is signed by the President of the United States."

Executive Mansion, July 5, 1865
The foregoing sentences in the cases of David E. Herold, G.A. Atzerodt, Lewis Powell aka Payne, Michael O'Laughlen, Edman Spangler, Samuel Arnold, Mary E. Surratt, and Samuel A. Mudd are hereby approved, and it is ordered that the sentences of said David E. Herold, G.A. Atzerodt, Lewis Payne, and Mary E. Surratt be carried into execution by the proper military authority, under the direction of the Secretary of War, on the 7th day of July 1865, between the hours of 10 o'clock a.m. and 2 o'clock p.m. of that day. It is further ordered that the prisoners, Samuel Arnold, Samuel A. Mudd, Edman Spangler, and Michael O'Laughlen be confined at hard

labor in the Penitentiary at Albany, New York, during the period designated in their respective sentences.
Andrew Johnson,
President

We silently read through the verdicts. The only one in our group to receive a shortened sentence was Ned Spangler—a reduction of six years. Samuel, Michael and I had been given life sentences for our roles in the assassination conspiracy.

I jerked in shock as my poor heart stiffened against this latest indignity. Forcing myself to continue, I read the details. The other conspirators had fared much worse: they would be *hanged by the neck until dead.*

We shot each other horrified looks, incredulous to have been judged so harshly and condemned so mercilessly.

Engulfed in misery, I dropped my head to my chest. A fine trembling began deep inside and soon spread from my stomach into my arms and legs.

Major General Hancock continued, a curious flatness to his voice. "You will soon be transferred to the federal penitentiary in Albany, New York."

I took a deep breath, trying to steady myself. "I want to see my wife before I leave," I said around the lump in my throat.

Hartranft looked over and nodded. "She has requested to see you and is waiting outside. We are providing her a pass from the State Department."

Relief flooded over me. "Today?" Again he nodded, turned stiffly to face Major General Hancock, and with a head nod the two stepped quickly out of the cell.

It would be several more days until my attorney explained how I missed the death sentence by just one vote. The Tribunal voted 5-4 to hang me, but a hanging sentence required a two-third majority of six votes. I was dumbstruck.

In less than an hour, General Dana's messenger arrived to take me to Frank. He stood by while I washed up and changed my clothing, then took me to a small room and left us alone.

Frank burst into tears when she saw me.

"My lovey, please. It will be all right," I told her, my voice splintering into my throat as I wrapped my arms around her and drew her close. Her hands were leaden and damp. Her mouth trembled and broke. She put her arms around me and fitted her face into the side of my neck, and I felt the heat of her tears. I gently stroked her back as she sobbed.

As I turned away to hide the tears slipping across my cheeks, I felt my blood racing through my veins as well as the thudding of my heart. My eyes shut tight with pain and despair.

Finally, she looked up into my face. "Oh Sammy, it's been so long. I am utterly lost without you, and now...prison...your life sentence. I cannot possibly bear this."

I led her gently to the chair and knelt beside her, calming her with soft words as I held her. I assured her I would write to President Johnson, giving him a convincing explanation of my innocence and pleading for an appeal.

Frank's head dropped toward her chest. "When I saw the men building the scaffold where the others were to be hanged, I was so frightened I would learn that you would be among them," she shuddered, her voice muffled as she swallowed hard to push back emerging tears. Then she looked down and saw my ankles.

"What happened to you? Are these from the chains? Is it painful?" She reached over to trace my bruises, her voice shaking.

I reassured her I was fine, then spoke tenderly of our children. "Frank, you must give them hope that I will be home soon. Speak well of me, so they won't forget their father." My words were choked with longing for the family now slipping away from me.

I clasped her frantically to my chest, closing the distance between us in this moment because tomorrow there would be so much more.

Frank looked into my eyes and tried to smile with her whole being, but her eyes remained glassy with tears. "I shall come to visit you in Albany, and perhaps I can even bring the children." Resting her face in her hands, I saw she was grasping for strength. "And I shall also go visit the President. I will tell him my side of the story."

The messenger walked in to return me to my cell. Frank's eyes were clear as she looked into mine. We spoke to each other through the calm silence that lay between us, then held each other tightly for one final moment. I felt my world slowing down and my senses heightening.

* * *

We were not moved from the Arsenal's Prison for the next few days. None of us asked for an explanation.

At 1 a.m. on July 17, 1865, a soldier woke us up and ordered us to get moving.

"What's going on?" I asked him.

"We're transporting you and the others today. Get your belongings together and put them in this bundle." He prodded us into action as he brought out the irons. "I have to put these back on you, so don't try to struggle," he grunted.

At 2:00 a.m., we groggily watched the *State Of Maine* pull away from the wharf and slip into the night. As dawn broke we were wide awake and unsure where we were going.

"Does anyone know where we are headed?" asked Sam Arnold, who seemed to be our self-appointed leader.

"Nay, but I think we're in the Chesapeake Bay," noted Michael O'Laughlen.

I stood quiet and pensive, wondering how I would be able to contact Frank and the children.

By mid-afternoon our ship had arrived at Fortress Monroe in Hampton, Virginia. We had crossed the Chesapeake and reached the point where it emptied into the Atlantic Ocean.

I later discovered that my wife read in the newspaper where we were headed even before I knew: we were going to the Dry Tortugas and the Fort Jefferson prison. The rest of us believed we were going to Albany until Arnold said we were sailing south.

15

JULY 26, 1865

My first letter to Frank was written aboard the *U.S.S. Florida* and mailed from Hilton Head, South Carolina, where we stopped for a day and a night. The officers invited a number of guests aboard for an evening of dancing and dining. Apparently relaxed and happy after their party, they decided to let us stay on deck for the rest of the trip. We were finally able to enjoy the cool breezes sweeping across the decks while we slept, without having to climb back into that stifling and smelly hold every night. As an additional gesture, the Captain ordered our chains removed during the daylight hours.

Once we were safely out to sea General Dodd told us our destination: the Dry Tortugas, Florida.

Our steamship was a 1,261-ton wooden side-wheel Navy ship used to help enforce the Atlantic coast blockade of Confederate shipping. It had also carried Union supplies down the Atlantic coast to the Gulf of Mexico, and transported Confederate prisoners to New York. Our commander, Captain William Budd, told us he'd been surprised by his orders to transport the convicted "Lincoln Assassination Conspirators."

In my letter to Frank, written at sea, I described our

original sleeping conditions, using a description Samuel Arnold had penned in his journal.

> *No sooner were we upon the gunboat than we were ordered into the lower hold of the vessel. It required, in our shackled condition, the greatest care to safely reach there, owing to the limited space, eight inches of chain allowed between our ankles. After leaving the second deck we were forced to descend upon a ladder whose rounds were distant so far apart that the chains bruised and lacerated the flesh and even the bones of our ankles. We remained in the sweltering hole during the night in an atmosphere pregnant with disagreeable odors, arising from various articles of subsistence stored within, and about 8 o'clock each morning we passed through another ordeal in our ascent to the deck, which was attended with more pain than the descent, owing to the raw condition of our wounds.*

On a brighter note I told her we were now sleeping on deck and our irons were removed during the day. I did not tell her what I still didn't know: in letters to the press the Dry Tortugas had been called "a perfect Hell," not because of its characteristics or weather, but because of its extremely limited space.

Several days before reaching Garden Key and the Dry Tortugas, my three friends and I struck up a conversation with Captain Budd about the island and its history. Our Captain was happy to flaunt his knowledge.

"Well, the fortress was built on this last lick of America—the Dry Tortugas—in 1846 for national defense," he began. "At first it defended the American waters from Caribbean pirates, but during the war it stayed with the Union and blockaded the Confederate ships from entering the Gulf of Mexico."

"Was it easy to find?" asked Michael O'Laughlen.

He shook his head and adjusted his control panel. "Nope, 'cuz it has five bastions jutting out of corners of a pentagon that guards an immense natural, almost invisible harbor."

We nodded, which he took as an affirmation to continue. "It was the only place for sixty miles where ships could sit out the hurricanes menacing the Gulf. Oh, and they could find protection under the Fort's guns in times of war."

I asked him, "Why did you say the harbor was invisible?

"Because its breakwaters, a great broken ring of coral, were submerged."

"How much action did the Fort see in the war?" asked Spangler, the historian of our group.

Captain Budd's eyes shone with amusement as he chuckled. "Not a damn bit of action! They realized the Fort would not withstand the new weapons of war." He looked sideways at us. "Imagine. Before its third tier was completed, the engineers discovered the weight of the massive structure was causing it to sink and they had to halt construction. Then the rifled cannon's invention meant that its seven-to-fifteen-foot thick walls were not thick enough to withstand attack."

The light in his eyes changed to an expression of dismay. "It was destined for glorious battle, but our Fort Jefferson sat out the war as a Union prison."

On the sixth day at sea, after our brief stop in South Carolina, a shout rose up: *"Land!"* We rushed forward to stare in awe as massive stone and brick walls gradually appeared out of the water, followed by green trees and a beautiful white, sandy beach on a scrap of sand no more than thirteen acres in total. Palm trees waved above it all, like graceful Japanese fans offered to royalty. Over the top of the Fort we saw the roof of a building with a tall, white lighthouse towering over everything.

This was our first glimpse of the end of the world: an enormous oven of glistening, blistering heat; a place without hope or amenities. The scenery was lovely but the Fort was grim, forbidding and entirely surrounded by a moat intended to keep enemies out and prisoners in. We quickly discovered that the waters encircling the Florida Keys were home to sharks and barracudas in search of floating snacks, making escape most unlikely.

We heard that there were not nearly as many people inhabiting the island now as during its peak time during the war, when the military population alone numbered 1,729. When we arrived there were 1,013 people living on the island: 486 soldiers and 527 prisoners, counting us. The prisoners' offenses included murder, man-slaughter, robbery, grand larceny and desertion. And the standing orders said: *"If a prisoner refuses to obey orders the sentinel must shoot him, and then use his bayonet, at the same time calling for the guard."* These words were imparted in our arrival briefing as we reported for duty.

We were given wooden planks to sleep on, and stretched out to get some rest. A vast bottomless fatigue slowly settled over me, like a great drifting net of cobwebs. Our hearts were heavy as we contemplated our new way of life, shut out from the world, where we would dwell and pass our remaining days. I decided at that moment that I would not accept that destiny. I would find a way to escape.

Dr. Samuel A. Mudd's Farm. *Photo by Frank M. Culhane, courtesy of the Dr. Samuel A. Mudd Society, Inc.*

Left, Sarah Frances Dyer before her wedding to Samuel A. Mudd. Right, Dr. Samuel A. Mudd before the conspiracy trial. *Photos courtesy of the Library of Congress.*

Dr. and Mrs. Samuel a. Mudd. *Courtesy of the Dr. Samuel A. Mudd Society, Inc.*

Dining Room at Dr. Samuel A. Mudd's home. *Courtesy of the Dr. Samuel A. Mudd Society, Inc.*

Parlor: the couch where John Wilkes Booth's leg was first examined. Checkerboard made by Dr. Mudd in Fort Jefferson. *Courtesy of the Dr. Samuel A. Mudd Society, Inc.*

Bedroom where John Wilkes Booth was treated for his broken leg. *Photo taken by author.*

The escape route from the Mudd farm to Zekiah Swamp. *Photo taken by author.*

Zekiah Swamp where Booth and Herold escaped. *Photo taken by author.*

The last photograph of Abraham Lincoln, April 10, 1865. *Photo by Alexander Gardner, Courtesy of the Library of Congress.*

The Ford Theatre, Washington City, circa 1865. *Courtesy of the L.C. Handy Studios.*

The single-shot Derringer that Booth used to kill President Lincoln. *Photo taken by author at the Ford Theatre.*

John Wilkes Booth, actor, Confederate sympathizer, assassin of President Lincoln. *Courtesy of the Edward Steers Jr. Collection.*

John Wilkes Booth's boot, cut by Dr. Samuel A. Mudd to set his broken leg. *Photo taken by author at the Ford Theatre.*

The President's box at the Ford Theatre. *Photo taken by author at the Ford Theatre.*

Mary E. Surratt. *Courtesy of the Surratt House Museum.*

The Surratt Boarding House. *Courtesy of the Surratt House Museum.*

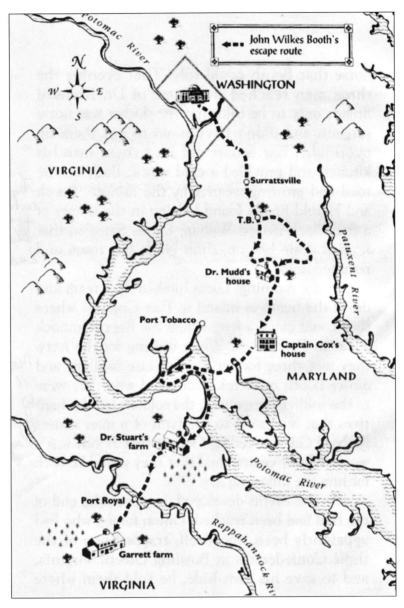

The dashed line shows John Wilkes Booth's escape rute following his assasination of President Lincoln on April 4, 1865. Historians are not certain which road was taken between the town of T.B., Maryland and Dr. Mudd's house. *Courtesy of the Surratt House Museum.*

Surratt House and Tavern. *Photo by Edward Steers, Jr. Courtesy of the Surratt House Museum.*

Anne Surratt. *Courtesy of the Surratt House Museum.*

John Harrison Surratt, Jr. *Courtesy of the Surratt House Museum.*

Guilty! Sentenced to hang (left column): Lewis Powell, David Herold, George Atzerodt and Mary Surratt (not pictured). Sentenced to prison (right column): Samuel Arnold, Ned Spangler, Michael O'Laughlen and Dr. Samuel Mudd (not pictured. *Courtesy of the Surratt House Museum.*

The Military Commission. Left to right: Col. Clendenim, Col. Tompkins Brig. Gen. Harris, Brig. Gen. Howe, Brig. Gen. Ekin, Major Gen. Wallace, Major Gen. Hunter, Major Gen. Kautz, Brig. Gen. Foster, Judge Bingham, Col. Burnett, Judge Holt. *Courtesy of the Library of Congress.*

The hanging of the conspirators. *Courtesy of the Library of Congress.*

The final judgement. Ten individuals found guilty by the government, four were sentenced to hang: Mary Surratt, Powell, Herold and Atzerodt. *Courtesy of the Library of Congress.*

Fort Jefferson—The Dry Tortugas. *Photo taken by author at Fort Jefferson.*

View of The Dry Tortugas Fort Jefferson prison. *Photo taken by author at the Dry Tortugas.*

Overview of Fort Jefferson on the Dry Tortugas. *Photo taken by author.*

Dr. Mudd's cell room, 2nd tier. *Photo taken by author.*

View from Dr. Mudd's cell. *Photo taken by author.*

President Johnson pardoned
Dr. Mudd on February 8, 1869.
Courtesy of the Library of Congress.

George St. Leger Grenfel. *Courtesy of Geocities Sites.*

Dr. and Mrs. Samuel A. Mudd's grave at St. Mary's Catholic Church in Bryantown, *Maryland. Photo taken by author.*

PART II

16

AUGUST 31, 1865

My first five weeks at Fort Jefferson have stretched into an eternity. It seems that each waking moment I am doing everything possible to survive while preserving my sanity. This is only feasible because of fond memories of the past; so I must keep them as clear and emotionally rich as I can. If only I could freeze them! Instead I feel them growing fainter by the hour, and with them my optimism for a peaceful future.

The morning after our arrival we were given a tour around the island, including Fort Jefferson's interior and exterior grounds. It was as baleful a tour as anyone might imagine, because of our shared terror of dying on this godforsaken speck in the sea.

Our first breakfast with the other prisoners consisted of weak coffee and bread speckled with bugs, dirt and even sticks. Then the four of us were turned loose to roam the grounds. The hot summer sun reflecting from the sand was so bright we squinted the whole time. The island's constant assault on our eyes eventually gives most of the prisoners "moon blindness"—almost complete loss of any night vision.

That morning we were given our numbers. Arnold

had become Prisoner 1523, O'Laughlen Prisoner 1525, Spangler Prisoner 1526 and I was Prisoner 1524. Then they handed out our assignments, based on our skills. Sam Arnold had attended Georgetown College so he would perform clerical duties in the office of the Fort's commanding officer. Ned Spangler would work in the carpentry shop. Mike O'Laughlen became a laborer helping with the ongoing construction of the Fort. And as a medical doctor, I was sent to the prison hospital.

Fort Jefferson's one entrance, the sally port, is situated in the southeast wall of the Fort. The gun rooms or casemates are located on the second tier of the sally port wall and serve as cells to house prisoners. My cell is behind the three rifle embrasures above the sally port entrance.

I desperately wanted to write a letter to my Frankie before evening arrived, which they allowed me to do. Everyone told us the mail was erratic, but I was quite surprised to learn that she did not receive that letter until after receiving three letters I had written at a later time.

In the meantime, Frank went to Washington City to meet with Secretary of War Stanton, asking him if she could send me money and clothing. She wrote me that he gazed at her in silence before answering her. "As long as Dr. Mudd is in prison, the government will furnish him with what it thinks necessary, and he can have no communication whatsoever with the outside world."

She was stunned, then infuriated. She wrote me that she fumed for three days before eventually receiving a letter from Secretary Stanton, written by E. D. Townsend, Assistant Adjutant-General. She read:

Madam: Your application of the 2d of August to know if you would be allowed to communicate with your husband, and if so by what means, and whether you are at liberty to send him clothing and articles of comfort and money, from home, has been considered by the Secretary of State. Dr. Mudd will be permitted to receive communications from you, if enclosed, unsealed, to the Adjutant-General of the Army at Washington. The government provides suitable clothing and all necessary subsistence in such cases, and neither clothing nor money will be allowed to be furnished him.

This first letter reached Frank after several other letters had arrived. There was no rhyme or reason to mail delivery: some letters never arrived at all. Fortunately the one dated August 24, 1865, did reach her. That letter was important because it enabled her to visualize my life in the Dry Tortugas.

Fort Jefferson, Dry Tortugas, FL
August 24, 1865
Dearest Frank,
Today one month ago we arrived here. Time passes very slowly and seems longer than that period, like years gone by. Sadly, I have received no news or letter whatever from home since being here. Some of the others who came with me have, but those letters contain no news and do not advert to the possibility or subject of release.
You know, my dear Frankie, that this subject is the all absorbing one of my mind. I worry that you or the little children are sick. Some may be dead, or some other mis-for-

tune has happened. Those questions frequently revolve in my mind and heart, and I worry that the dear ones at home are unwilling to break the cruel intelligence to me.

You know, were it not for you and those at home, I could pass the balance of my days here perfectly content or satisfied. Without you and the children, what is life for me—a blank, a void. If you have any regard for me, which I have never doubted, let me hear from you and often. I have written to you by every mail that has left this place, and surely some have been received. Mail sometimes arrives here in five days from New York.

This place continues to be unusually healthy, and the only fear manifested is that disease may be propagated by the arrival of vessels and steamers from infected ports. At this time there is a vessel lying at quarantine with all hands aboard sick with fever of some description. Several have died, and there is not one well enough to serve the sick. No volunteers from among the prisoners are going to them, so the chances of life are small.

I am working in the hospital. I have little or no labor to perform, but my fare is not much improved. My principal diet is coffee, butter and bread three times a day. We have had a mess or two of Irish potatoes and onions. Vegetables don't last many days in this climate before decomposition takes place. Pork and beef are poisonous to me; molasses when I am able to buy it, and occasionally fresh fish, when Providence favored, are the only articles of diet used. I am enjoying very good health, considering the circumstances.

Sweet, dearest Frankie, write to me soon on the receipt of my letter. I am afraid letters have been intercepted from either you or myself. If I don't hear from you soon, I am

*afraid I will become indifferent and careless. I have written
to Jere, Ewing, Stone, Ma and Papa some several letters—
others, one or two, and not one syllable have I received.*

*I am afraid when the silence is broken, the news will be
so great as to endanger our safety. My dear Frank, I have
nothing to interest you---several hundred prisoners have
been released and gone home recently to their families.*

*My anxiety increases upon the arrival of every boat
and mail, and I envy the departing homeward bound.
Give my love to all—kiss the children and believe me,
Truly and sincerely,
Your beloved husband, S.A. MUDD*

By the end of my first month in the Dry Tortugas, I
had fallen into what would become a regular debilitat-
ing cycle of rising hopes followed by hopeless descents
into deep despair. This week's arrival of uplifting letters
from family members, my attorney and well-meaning
friends provided a sense of courageous expectations of
imminent release. But then throughout the lonely sleep-
less nights that followed, the cell seemed to close in on
me and I plummeted into the depths of darkness and
despair. I wanted to simply give up and ask my family members to cease fighting for my case, but finally as
dawn broke I could not imagine abandoning my faith in
humanity, or in God.

Every day I managed to acquire some useful bit of
information or insight. Then in my cell waiting helplessly
for dawn, the uncertain promise of discovering some new
survival skill was sometimes all I needed to get up again
with fresh resolve.

My three friends and I discussed our mutual sense of deflation.

"Today I felt as if I'd been punched in the stomach," muttered Ned, sadness pulling down his features.

"Why? Did you receive bad news?" I asked.

He shook his head. "No, but I had a dream last night that a giant hand erased everything good that ever happened to me." His voice sliced. "I saw my heart shatter, cutting my soul, and the shards splintered into diamonds with sharp, unpolished edges."

At that moment, listening to my friend's pain, I desperately wanted to tear down everything, clear the landscape, and escape somewhere empty and clean.

Sam Arnold turned to Ned, and I felt the insides of my eyelids stinging. "Guess we can't bend our values to fit the times now, can we? Guess we'll just have to fit the times to our values," he said.

We watched the day come to life. Dawn was a rosy blush on the eastern sky, with hints of mauve just beneath. The air was already heating up, and it was only 6:00 a.m.

My weary eyes betrayed despair as my carefully maintained stoicism slipped away and I slumped against the rough wall.

"Don't despair, my friend," Ned told me, gently cooling my burning face with his palm. "We'll be okay."

I nodded slowly. My eyes closed, forcing the tears between the lids.

"Sam, look at me!" He lifted my face toward his. "You, of all of us, must keep a shadow of hope. That's all we have now."

17

The long conversation I had with General Dodd, Captain Budd and several others aboard the *U.S.S. Florida* has already been mentioned. That took place on the last leg of our trip to the Dry Tortugas. I spoke perhaps too freely to them about my three visits with John Wilkes Booth, because I felt that I no longer had anything to hide.

I could never have anticipated how much interest it would excite in the newspapers. The August 3rd edition of the *Washington Evening Star* featured an article based on a reporter's interview with General Dodd.

> *On the trip, Dr. Mudd acknowledged to Capt. Budd, Gen. Dodd and others that he knew Booth when he came to his house with Herold on the morning after the assassination, but that he was afraid to tell of his having been there, fearing the life of himself and family would be endangered thereby. He knew that Booth would never be taken alive.*

Unfortunately for me, that was *not* what I had actually told them, and I naturally felt angry and betrayed. I told them that because of his disguises I had never recognized Booth while attending to him in my home. I did admit to lying about having seen him on the two other occasions.

When Judge Advocate General Holt read the newspaper account he asked Captain George W. Dutton, who had led the guard detail aboard the ship, if I had actually said what the article claimed.

Dutton submitted an affidavit confirming the accuracy of the article. He added, *He also confessed that he was with Booth at the National Hotel on the evening referred to by Weichmann in his testimony, and that he came to Washington on that occasion to meet Booth by appointment, who wished to be introduced to John Surratt. I will also state that this confession was voluntary, and made without solicitation threat or promise, and was made after the destination of the prisoners was communicated to them. This affected Dr. Mudd more than the rest; he frequently exclaimed that there was now no hope for him.*

I was extremely disheartened and upset when I learned about this. I knew I must write a rebuttal, telling the whole truth. On August 28, 1865, I wrote my side of the story. Here are a few major annotations of this rebuttal to Judge Advocate General Holt.

*1st: That I confessed to having known Booth while in my house: was afraid to give information of the fact, fearing to endanger my life, or made use of any language in that connection—**I positively and emphatically declare to be notoriously false.***

2nd. *That I was satisfied and willingly acquiesced in the wisdom and decision of the Military Commission who tried me, is again notoriously erroneous and false.* **On the contrary, I charged the commission with irregularity, injustice, usurpation, and illegality.**

3rd. **I did confess to a casual meeting with Booth in front of one of the hotels on Pennsylvania Avenue, Washington City on the 23rd of December 1864, and not on January 15th.** *Booth wanted an introduction to Surratt, from whom he said he wished to obtain a knowledge of the country around Washington, in order to select a good locality for a country residence. I met Surratt and Weichmann, after which Booth insisted on going to his room to drink. I declined. After their insistence, I yielded, explaining I could stay only a few moments. Surratt and I stepped out into the hall and I apologized to him for having introduced Booth to him, since I knew so little about Booth. Later, Booth made me an offer to purchase my land, which I confirmed affirmatively, but heard no more about. I had no secret conversation with Booth, nor with Booth and Surratt together, as testified to by Weichmann. Booth's later visit in November was to purchase land and horses; he was inquisitive concerning the political sentiments of the people. He spoke greatly about his acting world, his father being a good Republican, his family business and many minor matters that caused me to suspect him to be a government detective and to advise Surratt regarding him.*

I never saw Mrs. Surratt in my life to my knowledge previous to the assassination, and then only through her veil. I never saw Arnold, O'Loughlen, Atzerodt, Payne alias Powell or Spangler—or ever heard their names mentioned previous to the assassination. I never saw or heard of Booth after the 23rd of December 1864, until after the assassination, and then he was in disguise and I did not recognize him. Neither Booth's nor Herold's name was mentioned in connection with the assassination, nor were there any names mentioned on the Tuesday after the assassination, nor was there any photograph exhibited of any one implicated in the infamous deed.

The Friday after the assassination, when Lieutenant Lovett and his cavalry came to my farm, I remembered the boot I had cut from Booth's leg and, without hesitation, I handed it to Lieutenant Lovett. They read his name inside the boot and showed me his photograph, asking if it bore a resemblance to the party, to which I said I could not recognize that as the injured man, but remarked there was a resemblance about the eyes and hair. I saw no resemblance in the photograph of Herold either, but I described the horse upon which he rode, which was the same horse that was taken from the stable. I then formed a judgment, and expressed it without hesitation. I said I was convinced that the injured man was Booth, the same man who visited my house in November 1864, and purchased a horse from my neighbor, George Gardiner. I said this because I thought my judgment in the matter was necessary to secure pursuit promptly of the assassins.

After sending my rebuttal to the proper authorities, I waited and hoped to receive a response. In the meantime, in the past few days the control of Fort Jefferson was transferred from the 161st New York Volunteers to the 82nd U.S. Colored Infantry. Up to this time we had received good treatment under the 161st; but now, as a recent slave owner and a person convicted of conspiring to kill the president who had freed the slaves, I became worried.

The officers of the U.S. Colored Infantry were fine-looking men and the privates, mostly from Mississippi and Louisiana, appeared to be stalwart healthy soldiers. They were constantly frolicking and playing games and tricks on each other. We soon understood how proud they were to be soldiers. After several weeks of interacting with them, we knew they were good and decent men.

Nevertheless, I realized the time had come to orchestrate my escape, in case it should become necessary to run.

18

Thirty or forty prisoners had successfully escaped during the two months we'd been at the Dry Tortugas. Most found freedom by stowing away on one of the steamer ships that bring supplies to the island. For example, one steamer, the *Thomas A. Scott*, recently sailed away with eight hidden prisoners. Contemplating various escape strategies, this one seemed to be the most likely to succeed.

I had to be clever to avoid any suspicion prior to engaging my plans. I did not share my ideas with anyone, not even my three friends. Knowing that my mail was read by my captors before being transmitted, I chose to write a letter to my wife openly denouncing the idea of escaping, timing it shortly before the next expected arrival of the *Thomas A. Scott*.

> *I have had several opportunities to make my escape, but knowing, or believing, it would show guilt, I have resolved to remain peaceable and quiet, and allow the Government the full exercise of its power, justice and clemency. Should I take "French leave," it would amount to expatriation, which I don't feel disposed to do at present.*

Because Fort Jefferson is such an isolated prison, the inmates were granted greater liberties of freedom than at other prisons. When I wasn't working as a nurse in the hospital, I was allowed almost complete access to the island. We were all expected to sleep within the walls of the Fort, but we did not have bed check, and the only days we were watched closely were the days that ships departed the island. During those times, we were forbidden to leave the grounds of the Fort until the ship had sailed.

The day before the *Thomas A. Scott* was due to arrive, I slept outside the Fort in the shed. Several of my fellow inmates had done this before. On September 25th, I changed my clothing from prisoner garb to one of the suits I had brought with me.

While the crew was unloading supplies, I befriended a young crew member named Henry Kelly and asked him for his help. This was a serious risk because if he turned me in, I would be severely punished. So I persuaded him by offering a nice payment. He agreed to hide me and care for me during my escape.

During the great activity and transfer of supplies on and off the ship, I was able to slip down into the lower hold near the coal bunkers and hide myself under a platform between two cross beams. Henry Kelly suggested that would be the safest place, and said he would find me there after the ship put out to sea.

To my everlasting regret, I was recognized by one of the Fort's officers as I boarded the ship. Had I been a lowly thief or murderer I do not believe that the military storekeeper, who was overseeing the removal of supplies, would have recognized me. But we four Lincoln conspirators did not have the anonymity of a common criminal. Mr. Jackson promptly reported to the post commander that "Dr. Mudd went down below and has not come up again."

A patrol quickly assembled and spread throughout the ship, probing into every nook and cranny large enough to conceal a human. The search was on. I was lying under a box in the coal bunker and prayed they would not find me.

I held my breath as the heavy boots drew near. My sense of hearing and smell seemed to heighten as I clearly heard the smelly water sloshing in the darkness below me. My ears rang—a certain sign of fear. A great deal of shouting was taking place in the passageways above and I began to feel dizzy, but clung tightly to the slippery supports in the hold. I closed my eyes and kept praying, thinking of my family and the joy of embracing every one of them.

Suddenly, I heard a peculiar sound. It was the sound of a saber slicing through the box. I knew the cold steel would come into contact with my body. Terrified, I cried out and told them I would come out peacefully.

I stumbled back off the ship smutty, discomfited and completely crestfallen. They twisted my arms behind me and dragged me topside, shouting out their success. I knew they would take me to Major George E. Wentworth, my now very angry commanding officer. His eyes flashed with suppressed fury as he jabbed a finger toward my chest and weighed my punishment.

Naturally I was immediately re-arrested and interrogated. Grilling me, they asked about O'Laughlen, Arnold and Spangler. I told them they knew nothing of my escape and after a quick search, the three men were found inside the walls.

I refused to give up my accomplice and that stoked their anger even more. After two hours of my obstinacy, they threatened to shoot me, and I believed they would. Despondently, I gave them his name. Regrettably, Henry Kelly was imprisoned as the ship left the island. They so rejoiced at finding me that they did not care to look any further. That afternoon the *Thomas A. Scott* departed with four other prisoners, who, for all I know, made good their escape.

Because I had attempted to escape, I was put in the guardhouse with chains on my hands and feet, and closely confined for two days. Then the Major sent the order to put me into hard labor, pushing sand in a wheelbarrow. My new boss had me cleaning old bricks. The order also directed the Provost Marshal to closely confine me on the arrival and departure of every steamer.

Deeply saddened and guilt-ridden about my betrayal of Henry Kelly, I wrote a note to the commander taking full responsibility for my escape attempt and stated that, although Kelly had promised to help me escape, he actually took no part in it. He was unloading supplies while I entered the steamer. I begged the commander to release him, or at least transfer him to the authorities in nearby Key West. I insisted that as a civilian Kelly should not be imprisoned here with me.

To the Major Commander
Sir:
I acknowledge to having acted contrary to my own judgment and honor, in my attempted escape. I assure you it was more from the impulse of the moment and with the

hope of speedily seeing my disconsolate wife and four little infants. Mr. Kelly did not secrete me aboard, but only promised to do so. Before I was detected I had made up my mind to return if I could do so without being observed by the guards. I am truly ashamed of my conduct, and if I am restored again to the freedom of the Fort and former position, no cause shall arise to create your displeasure. And, I shall always counsel subordination to the ruling authorities. By complying or relieving me from my present humble locality—you will merit the gratitude of your humble servant, a devoted wife and four dear little children. I do not complain of the punishment, but I feel that I have abused the kindness and confidence reposed, and would be glad exceedingly to comply with any other honorable acquirement, whereby, I may be able to wash away the folly of my weakness.
TRULY & RESPECTFULLY YRS,
SAML. A MUDD

While the commander was waiting on instructions for Henry Kelly, he decided to house him in the guardhouse with me.

"Kelly, your incarceration here is infuriating!" I told him emotionally. "And it's all my fault. I should never have asked this favor of you."

The young man smiled, reaching over to squeeze my shoulder. "They will not keep me long. I think they cannot legally hold me on the island. My superiors will send the order to release me." His voice sounded so young.

"Can you forgive me?" I asked, drawing in a slow, deep breath. "I do not deserve it, but can you?"

He nodded, and offered me his hand.

Five days later, he was taken to the "dungeon," a place much worse than where we were. His housemate was a thief named Smith. Both were clad in wrist and ankle chains. Yet, somehow they broke out of the iron grated window in their cell. They lowered themselves down by using the same chains, then quietly moved on to rob the island's civilian merchant of 50 dollars, some clothing and enough canned foods to last their journey. Under the cover of darkness, they put out to sea in a small boat.

With an enormous smile, I commented to the man who guarded me, "The authorities are no doubt much disappointed and chagrined at this unexpected act. I, however, feel much relieved. Justice has been served."

19

OCTOBER 30, 1865

On October 18th, the other Lincoln conspirators and I were sent to the "dungeon" that Kelly had escaped from. The rumor of a plot to free the four conspirators had reached the Secretary of War so he alerted his divisional commanders in the south. General Phil Sheridan ordered a lieutenant to inform every unit in Florida to report any suspicious activities. Naturally, we were considered to be involved so they quickly confined us all to the Fort's most secure cell.

Our living quarters worsened considerably in the dungeon. For one thing, we were not alone. The floor was littered with a group of chained former Confederate soldiers. One was possibly the most colorful man to have ever worn a Rebel uniform.

Colonel George St. Leger Grenfel—a British citizen in his fifties born in Penzance, Cornwall, England—was a well-known soldier of fortune. Under his battered appearance was a man to be reckoned with, who was actively planning his escape. I quickly learned how deceiving looks can be.

His faded-out watery blue eyes missed nothing as he stretched his thin muscular figure to closely examine the newcomers. His long, graying hair and leathery skin were almost as dirty as an open red flannel shirt that gave him the appearance of a bandit. He had a lean, skull-like face, partially concealed by a finely pointed gray-brown beard, completely unkempt. He moved with the disjointed grace of a marionette.

It took him only a few minutes to acquaint us with his astonishing adventures.

"I ran away from home at a very young age," he began, speaking in a deep, melancholy voice. "I believe I was just seventeen then. I joined the French Foreign Legion to fight the Riffs and Tuaregs in North Africa, then went on down to South America to serve under Giuseppe Garibaldi. I spent about three years in a French lancer regiment and rose from private to second lieutenant."

The four of us could only listen in awe, held captive by his soothing, deep voice and the story of his life.

"A few years later I went to India and helped put down the Sepoy Mutiny, joining the British Army for the Crimean War against the Russians."

I asked when he had come to the United States.

"Well now, after the American War began I was back in England, living the life of a country gentleman. But I became bored with that life, so at the outset of your Civil War I told my friends that if England was not at war I would go elsewhere to find one, and I did. I decided to cast my lot with the Confederates and offered my services to General Robert E. Lee, who put me to work running the Federal blockade. General Braxton Bragg had me commissioned Inspector General and I served briefly with John Hunt Morgan's Raiders."

Ned Spangler was incredulous. "What did you do for Morgan?"

Throwing back his head, Grenfel roared with laughter. "Lee sent me to Morgan's headquarters with this request: 'Give Grenfel every opportunity to gratify his rather extraordinary appetite for hazardous adventures.'"

We joined him in laughter and urged him to continue.

He did. "I was placed on Morgan's staff with the post of Adjutant-General. He wanted to pay me but I was receiving enough money from England to live in the style I was accustomed to, so I told him to give it to the soldiers. I trained Confederate troops in cavalry tactics and horsemanship. Later, I fought alongside those same boys in battle, often on the front line."

Ned waited a moment, then asked, "How long were you with him? And where did you go next?"

"Let me think...hmm. To answer your first question, I chose December 20th to take leave of Morgan and his men. I knew Morgan was reorganizing his troops and I wanted command of the Brigade, but he gave it to William Breckinridge, who despised me. The feeling was mutual, so I sought out Bragg and became Inspector of Cavalry of the Army of Tennessee."

Watching us closely, he continued with a shrug. "Next, I went to Richmond and sought out General "Jeb" Stuart, who appointed me Assistant Inspector-General of the Corps of Cavalry of the Army of Northern Virginia. Unfortunately, my time there was brief as we did not see eye to eye on Stuart's careful observance of military formalities."

Grenfel paused, drawing in a long breath. "After a few more adventurous trips I landed in Washington City, where I convinced Secretary of War Edwin M. Stanton that I was retired from the Confederate Army and wanted to provide information about the Confederacy in exchange for free travel in the north. I thought spying would suit me well. So I agreed to take part in a grandiose scheme to split the Union in half and force Congress or the President to sue for peace." His eyes twinkled at his reminiscences.

"According to the plan, Confederate undercover agents would break into northern prison camps in Ohio, Indiana, Illinois, Michigan and Wisconsin and form a Northwestern Confederacy. They would free the 15,000 southern soldiers held captive and help them destroy or capture a number of major midwestern cities."

Sam O'Laughlen commented drily, "That didn't go according to plan, did it?"

"No, indeed it did not," answered Grenfel. "Thanks to one of Lafayette Baker's spies, I was betrayed. The Secret Service discovered what was happening. They also rounded up another one hundred fifty of the plotters before they could carry out their assignments. I was one of them."

I shook my head in sorrow, thinking of our fate. Why did the wrong people end up in chains?

"I was arrested in Chicago and stood trial in Cincinnati. I was sentenced to be hanged in April of this year," he stated, looking directly at me as he spoke. "Because I am a British citizen, and since they were flooded with letters from across the Atlantic, President Andrew Johnson decided not to rock the international boat. He simply cancelled the execution and ordered me to be moved down here."

And yet, the President cannot be bothered to do anything for us, his own citizens, I thought bitterly. *Perhaps he sent Grenfel into our lives to renew our hope, and teach us how to persevere. No, that would have been God.*

"When did you get here?" Sam Arnold asked him.

"Arrived on October 8 and got tossed right here into the dungeon. Heard all about you boys before you came in to join me," he grinned.

"Are you here for life?" I asked.

He nodded. "Unless we find a way out, or the good Lord decides otherwise. Like you four, I'm considered a 'state prisoner.' I believe we're all in this together because the good doctor here attempted escape, and the men in charge fear we will commit an uprising if allowed more freedom."

I bowed my head in shame. Now four other men were depending on me to avoid bringing more punishment down on all of us by trying another escape.

"I am a physician, as you know," I told him. "I believe you are suffering with dropsy, or edema. Are you allowed medical treatment?"

"No, I am not. But with the food we are fed here, I do not expect to recover anyway."

"What you need first is to have those chains, which are causing obstruction in the blood vessels, removed from your arms and legs. Does the swelling of your legs and ankles pain you?"

He shrugged. "I take no notice of it, as I know there is no solution."

I was not finished. "Let me see if I can get you something from the hospital. I worked there for a while, and I will try to speak with the doctor about it."

And thus began my remarkable alliance with Colonel George St. Leger Grenfel.

20

The only benefit to being locked away in this rank and dimly lit dungeon is that it provides me more time to write letters to my family. Imagining a conversation with them helps ease the gnawing pain of separation and improves reflection on my life in prison for a meager sense of personal growth and new insight. And as difficult as this might seem, there are other prisoners here in more dire straits than I, and my hope is to find a way to help them.

For example, three days ago I wrote to my brother-in-law Jeremiah Dyer asking him to contact the British Ambassador in Washington, Sir F.A. Bruce, to see about assisting Grenfel. I explained how impressed I was with my newfound friend and how he was suffering from treatable wounds and disease, lack of medical treatment, the burden of weighty chains and our loathsome food. I warned Jere that if something were not done to help this man soon, he would die.

To my dear Frank, I wrote letters of love, hope and longing.

My darling wife,
When I am capable of beholding with a serene eye the

mild and beneficent sway of the Fathers of the Republic, and the former prestige of the American Flag, then I shall calmly and patiently submit to this present degradation. You need have no further apprehension regarding my conduct. I have not had a cross word with an individual, soldier or prisoner, since I have been closeted upon this island of woe and misery. I have striven to the utmost of my ability to render myself and those around me comfortable, visiting the sick, and saving my scanty means to the last dime. To bear patiently under such circumstances requires more than human strength. I trust my present good resolutions will be supported by grace from above, through the prayerful mediation of you and all.

Since my effort to get away, eleven have made good their escape, all of whom were sentenced for a long period of years. My heart almost bleeds when I think of you and our dear little children, and the many pleasant hours we used to enjoy together. I feel they will be too large for me to handle when I shall be a free man again, and be able to return to you. My love and devotion appears to increase with every day. Give my love to all, Ma, Pa, and the family, and tell them to write. I am consoled by every letter. I don't wish you to write anything that may have a tendency (if made public) to be detrimental to my cause. Exercise prudence.

Goodbye, my sweet, precious wife and dear little ones. God bless you all.
Yours, etc.
S.M.

The dungeon's earlier occupants quickly accepted our group. They liked having a doctor close at hand and were excited to learn that Arnold and O'Laughlen had also served in the Confederate Army.

It didn't take long for the former comrades-in-arms to begin sharing anecdotes about where they had served and the rough and tumble of fighting for a losing cause. Soon we were getting along famously with Grenfel and the others.

As I mentioned earlier, we had been transferred to the dungeon because it was considered the most secure cell in the Fort. It featured a locked wooden door, a slate floor, slimy wet brick walls and two gun ports. Since only one port was left open (the other locked tightly with metal shutters), we had no cross ventilation. The room was choked with shadows and fetid gloom.

The little bit of sunlight that managed to fall through this single port made the floor beneath it a popular meeting place for conversation; we could imagine the small opening of blue sky was a familiar outdoor spot from our pasts.

To make matters worse, just outside our small open port was the area where the Fort's toilets, called sinks, emptied into the 70-foot-wide moat just underneath it. The architects must have assumed the moat would be flushed clean by ocean tides, but that was seldom the case. As a doctor I knew that the moat's aroma was more than merely nasty and unbearably foul; it was also filled with very dangerous sulphuric hydrogen gas, highly injurious to our health.

Slowly, the bad food and living conditions began to affect everyone's health. Scurvy was a major medical problem, due to the lack of fruits and vegetables containing vitamin C. I think Sam Arnold and I are suffering from rheumatism, and I suddenly feel as if I am losing weight. When I look into a mirror, I scarcely recognize myself.

Colonel Grenfel and I soon discovered how much we had in common: along with being quite stubborn and with hot tempers, we were also very determined to achieve our goals. As you might imagine, such qualities did not endear us to the authorities running Fort Jefferson.

Now we must spend all day in chains. Closely guarded, we may not leave the rest of the group unless escorted by a guard armed with musket and bayonet. Six days a week we are let out of the dungeon to work at hard labor. On Sundays and holidays we are confined all day inside the noxious cell.

At least the leg irons are removed whenever we are inside the dungeon.

Colonel Grenfel's spirit of prickly defiance has become his defining characteristic. He seems to have taken pains to be conspicuously disorderly, and the more menial his duties were, the more one saw of him.

"I say old bean," he would shout to one of the somnolent guards, "is this where I should be piling the dirt? In this corner, or perhaps that one?" Then he would stride back and forth inspecting each dim corner with a lordly air, a scraggly broom hoisted over one shoulder like a Viking inspecting his troops with a battle axe.

His merry impertinence was more than just about directly irritating our jailers; as our only form of entertainment it helped us maintain hope and resolve, resisting the officials' attempts to break our spirits and be more compliant.

In spite of my efforts to stay strong and healthy, I realized that I was suffering mentally and physically. My legs and ankles were swollen and sore, and I experienced pains in my back and shoulders. My hair began falling out so I shaved it all off. My eyesight concerned me when I recently realized it had become difficult to read or write by candlelight.

"Ned, are you ill?" I asked my friend softly, hearing his weak moans from a foot away.

"It's the food, I believe. I was so hungry I ate some of the rotten meat mixed with the fish," he whimpered. "I cannot stomach it much longer."

Colonel Grenfel was also awake. "Sam, do you understand why neither you nor I have been taken out to work the past three days?"

"Probably due to something they read in my incoming mail." I knew my Uncle Thomas Dyer had written to Major-General Sheridan to forward me some clothing and money. So far I had received nothing, but most likely the correspondence and responding package had been intercepted.

As we settled down again into familiar hopeless silence, I closed my eyes and fell into an equally familiar state of deep despondency. A sudden wave of sorrow swallowed me and squeezed burning tears from under my eyelids and across my cheeks.

21

I wrote to Frank and my parents on Christmas Day to let them know I was well and how much I missed everyone. My heart was heavy as I contemplated the Christmas holiday away from them and the bitter problems I was continuing to heap on them.

For example, Jere had written that it had become necessary to rent out the farm, and I felt this loss as deeply as if I had personally done this myself. One reason I had become a doctor was because of my sincere desire to make people feel better and help them overcome pain. Given the consequences of past decisions, I began to feel as if I had abandoned my Hippocratic Oath.

I frequently wonder what I have done to bring so much trouble upon my family. Knowing the answer is "nothing," I can only console myself a little with the knowledge that it is God's will and the greatest of His saints achieved their sanctity after facing the most painful travails willingly and even gratefully.

So I will do whatever I can to console Frank and our beloved children during these dark hours of our lives, even from afar.

As a practicing Catholic, I was saddened and concerned

that I hadn't attended Mass or received communion since arriving at Fort Jefferson. I recite my rosary every day and have tried to follow the religious training I received as a boy. I even shared a prayer with Frankie that God would bring us back together in this life; or if not now, in the next.

I was told that my wife and relatives were writing and visiting President Johnson with requests for my release. That kept me going through the month of December, and the joy I received on the 22nd of December was a blessed Christmas gift.

The President finally issued an order for better treatment to those of us in the dungeon. We were relieved of our chains and later moved from the dungeon to better quarters on January 26th. I believe that was due to Frankie's persistence through her letters.

My belief in the importance of outside pressure wasn't shared by all in our group. As we waited at the dungeon door for the escort taking us to the new quarters, I gave thanks to God and our families and friends for the increased comfort and freedom we had been granted.

Sam Arnold scoffed at my earnest appraisal in a friendly way.

"That order was probably issued a week ago and mislaid by a clerk somewhere."

O'Laughlen rolled his muscular shoulders and growled: "They just came to their senses and realized we weren't no threat to nobody."

Ned shrugged and spread his feet. "No matter how it came together, don't it feel fine to take big steps again?"

Grenfel turned and muttered so our guard couldn't

hear him. "Aye, and without those blasted chains it will be that much easier to put this rock behind us for good." Apparently he still harbored some dream of escape.

Through Christmas we were still waiting for a visit by a priest; I yearned to go to confession and communion and meet all the requirements of our holy religion.

Suddenly my prayers were answered! On December 28th, Bishop Augustine Verot of Savannah, Georgia arrived with the Rev. Father James O'Hara from Key West, Florida and requested to see me.

Bishop Verot had been assigned previously to a parish in Clarksville, Maryland and worked primarily with poor slaves. He spoke glowingly to me of his personal joy in having led them to Christ. He later shared with us that during the international meeting of bishops and cardinals, known as Vatican Council I, he had spoken out of the need for Catholics to seek reconciliation with Protestants and had asked church members to stop interfering in matters of purely scientific research. Now he was on a more pressing mission—to bring God's message to an island long deprived of any vestige of hope or faith.

Dressed in my best—and as always surrounded by guards—I attended Mass and visited with the pastors.

Father O'Hara listened with a concerned expression as I described our conditions in the dungeon and how my faith and ability to hope had been so frequently tested.

"Remember this dungeon is like the lions' den where Daniel was sent as punishment for publicly proclaiming his faith," Father O'Hara reminded me.

"The lions' mouths were shut by God so Daniel escaped any harm. In the same way He gives you strength to gracefully overcome your many privations and tribulations. Here is something more that will help you."

He handed me a letter written by my cousin Ann containing a small ivory crucifix, a scapular and a few other items. Grasping these to my breast, I joyfully participated in Holy Mass.

That same afternoon I attended a lecture given by the Bishop, then was allowed the privilege of confession. The next morning, just before their departure, I had the satisfaction and fulfillment of taking communion and receiving his personal blessing.

I have now resolved that I have but one affliction: uneasiness of mind regarding my wife and children. Imprisonment, chains and all other accompaniments of prison life I can endure. My constant prayer is that God be merciful to us and grant me a speedy release and safe return to my family.

* * *

Finally released from the dungeon, we were told that our former "soft jobs" were gone: I could not return to the hospital and Sam Arnold was no longer needed in the provost marshal's office.

We were given the exhausting chore of scraping and stacking bricks in the hot sun for the Fort construction. When Grenfel, O'Laughlen and Spangler joined me, we pledged privately to do our work as instructed but at our own pace.

The day was perfect. The sky was an inverted bowl of cerulean blue. The recent rains had scrubbed it to a high shine, and puffy white clouds crossed its arc in an orderly formation.

To avoid playing the model prisoner role for our guards, we spent entire days cleaning just one brick apiece.

It began with Colonel Grenfel, and as usual by taunting the authority figures closest at hand—our guard detail.

After the sergeant in charge told us what to do and marched away self-importantly, the Colonel picked up the nearest brick and thoughtfully hefted it as if testing its weight just before heaving it. The guard glanced around nervously and took two steps backward, his eyes fixed on the brick in Grenfel's hand.

Then the Colonel turned to us and in a crude imitation of the sergeant's gruff manner barked out: "Dash it, boys! You heard him. Scrape one brick and stack it right there, carefully now."

He slowly scraped the brick with a stick and after giving it some spit polish with his little finger, he let the brick drop to his side and raised his face skyward—apparently counting clouds.

After wasting a good twenty minutes in this manner, he sauntered over to the stack of bricks and slowly tipped it onto another brick, taking care to make certain the bricks were in clean alignment.

Finally he leaned wearily on the stack and turned to me, as if making polite chatter before tea in Buckingham Palace: "You never told me, old chap, which bugs you prefer in your bread—the tiny seedy ones or the flat ones with that satisfying crunch?"

Soon we were all entertaining ourselves with variations of his performance at the expense of our long-suffering guard. In hindsight, it's remarkable how easily our group of God-fearing formerly law-abiding citizens had begun subverting prison authority. Was this because we didn't feel we deserved the hard judgments meted out by the court? Or perhaps an unspoken need to feel like men unfortunate enough to be imprisoned?

Whatever the reason, the pleasure we received from resisting the officials' intent had memorable repercussions.

They took Grenfel away, thinking he was the instigator of our obstinacy. They chained a thirty-pound ball to his leg and told him to unload coal. He obeyed until his body began to collapse.

"I cannot do this, Sir," he told his boss. "My body will not tolerate the stress."

The heavy-set guard grunted, "If you do not work, you will not eat."

Colonel Grenfel looked him directly in the eyes and stood his ground. Time passed without a word from either one.

The others and I watched enraged as they tied him to a grate outside the prison walls where the sun beat down on him all day. His hands were tied over his head while his feet were fastened to a rope on the ground. The flies and mosquitoes buzzed and bit him, but not even that could break the older man's spirit.

At the end of the day, the Irish Lieutenant Robinson—acting Provost Marshal—ordered the guard to take Grenfel to the nearby wharf. He was laid down on the wharf where they removed his chains, but tied his hands savagely behind him so as to cut the skin around his wrists. They threw him into the Gulf of Mexico.

Handicapped by the ropes, Grenfel struggled to the surface and managed to keep his head above water. He used his legs to tread water, and when the Lieutenant saw that he ordered the soldiers to bind Grenfel's legs and toss him back into the water. Smirking at the spectators, Grenfell floated on his back.

"Haul him back in and add weights to his legs," growled Lieutenant Robinson.

Six men pulled him back onto the wharf and added weights to his legs. Of course he sank to the bottom, twenty feet deep, and began drowning.

"Raise him back up," shouted Robinson.

Grenfel was pulled up, sputtering and gasping.

"Now will you work?"

Grenfel shook his head.

Thrice more he was thrown back into the water until fainting from the seawater that now filled his lungs. The Lieutenant kicked him back to consciousness, viciously stripping skin from his ribs, elbows and hands with his boot's toes. He then walked away from the soggy, inert piece of flesh and blood.

A kindly guard sneaked out during the night, untied him and brought him inside. He was able to revive him with hot liquids and a blanket.

We did not see him until the next morning when we participated in reveille and inspections. Lieutenant Robinson finished his breakfast and headed for the main gate leading out of the prison. He was met with an amazing apparition.

Standing before him was the man he had left for dead. Wet, filthy, bruised, battered and cut, Colonel Grenfel snapped sharply to attention.

Completely humiliated and shamed, the Lieutenant

spoke nervously. "Going to pick up those bricks now, Grenfel?"

There was a long silence. Grenfel stared at him: eyes locked, unmoving.

Grenfel slowly shook his head. Lieutenant Robinson broke. Grunting something under his breath, he stepped around the beaten man and walked away.

22

MARCH 3, 1866

The letters from home arrived more frequently now. I was beginning to put together the pieces of the puzzle of my family's lives as well as where they were in their efforts to secure my freedom.

I insisted that Jere give me details of the family's situation, so he reluctantly recounted horrific details of Frankie's treatment after my arrest. The soldiers who arrested me had returned to my farm the following day in case Booth returned. His failure to appear made them so angry they burned the fences, destroyed our crops and pulled apart a storehouse, which spilled all our ears of corn onto the ground. They even broke open our meat house and stole the contents while threatening servants who tried to stop them. Poor Frankie was roughly searched for food she might be carrying to Booth.

Jere also told me about the afternoon when troops outside the house shouted rude threats and insults at my wife inside. She put the children to bed, pulled down the curtains and locked the doors. Shortly after midnight, she heard a loud knocking and believed the end was nigh. But it was her cousin Sylvester, who had sneaked through the picket lines to protect her and the children. They stayed up talking until dawn to keep up their courage.

"I am so frightened, Sylvester. I feel as though I should die of anxiety when the soldiers arrive."

"Do not concern yourself with them, Frank, but rather, keep your calm bearing for the children. Your family will protect you."

The very next morning the troops received the news that Booth had been located, and they quickly departed our farm. My wife had written none of this to me so I wouldn't be anxious during the trial.

Another time a Lieutenant rode to the farm announcing he had come to take Frank into town for questioning. She said she had important chores to attend to and would ride in the following day. The Lieutenant agreed and rode away in a rapid cloud of dust.

The next morning she and her brother Jere took a stage into Washington City, where they were met by a cavalry unit and escorted to Lafayette Baker's office. They spoke with him and he asked her to return the following day. Frankie shared with him her concern for our children at home, and he told her to wait around to hear from him by 2:00 p.m.

"If you hear nothing from me by then, you are free to return home." Lafayette Baker was impressed with this woman. "I will look after your concerns," he assured her.

That afternoon Frank and Jere left, without ever discovering why they were summoned in the first place.

After my conviction Frank continued to organize the legal paperwork and run errands to support my case. Finally granted an audience with the President, she pleaded with him to pardon me—unaware that Johnson was fighting his own impeachment due to his disagreements with Secretary of War Stanton.

To protect himself, the President told Frank he could only release me if the War Department agreed. So my poor wife returned to Stanton's headquarters and spoke with Judge Advocate General Holt. He told her there was nothing he could do.

Jere then contacted ex-Governor Thomas H. Ford, a defender of the underdog and an enemy of Lafayette Baker. Ford was very impressed with Jere's presentation and returned to speak with President Johnson, who reluctantly promised he would release me as soon as he "could," adding that he didn't believe I should have been jailed in the first place.

My trial by the military commission turned out to be flagrantly unconstitutional. Less than a year after it occurred, on April 3, 1866, the Supreme Court handed down such a ruling in the case of Lambdin P. Milligan, one of Colonel Grenfel's associates. Naturally, that decision did me no good. Stanton was out for blood and had no intention of releasing the four of us serving our time at Fort Jefferson.

Being completely cut off from civilization, I wasn't aware of everything being done on my behalf and could only fret between letters. So in one long letter I did what the average sinful man would do—I cruelly took out my frustration on the least deserving person. I chastised Frankie for writing me only twice a month without answering my questions; criticized her for promising to come to visit me when she knew she could not; lambasted her for rarely telling me what was going on at home; and even censured her grammar and penmanship. *I have received several letters that I could not read nor understand because your words were spelled backwards or had a whole syllable left out. How do you expect me to answer your letters when I can scarcely read them?*

My words were cruel and must have hurt her deeply. I regretted them the moment I mailed that letter.

In my next letter, and in the following one written days later, I apologized for my harsh language and asked for her forgiveness. I told Frank I had ignored how hard she worked with the children and begged her to take care of her health. I warned her to be careful of prowlers after one of our neighbors had been murdered and another had been robbed. I begged her to hire someone to help with the farm work.

In my free moments, I quickly crafted some little gifts I had learned to make: large moss-cards, a cross, a wreath, and a crabwood cane, which I sent her, as well as a handful of shells I found on the lonely night beach walks. I was surprised at how quickly I picked up the skill of carpentry from others who worked in the shop. Ned Spangler was very helpful and encouraged me in this work.

Somehow Frank comprehended what really bothered me and caused my callousness. It was the fact that I knew I was innocent of my charges. The only thing I had done was set a patient's broken leg.

In an attempt to write her gentler news, I sent this letter in early March.

Art often overcomes and subdues nature. My disposition is undergoing a change. The virtue of resignation to an adverse and unjust punishment is rapidly dying out within me, and a different spirit supplanting. God knows I try to control these emotions, but it seems almost in vain.

History often reverses itself. Pilate, fearing the displeasure of the multitude, condemned our Lord to death. Is not mine somewhat an analogous case? Owing to the excitement and influence prevailing at the time of my trial, I could excuse much; but since time has elapsed for a sober, dispassionate consideration of the matter, I am becoming vexed at my protracted exile. I suppose it is all human.

I am truly grieved to hear of Mother's bad health—would that I could prescribe something to cure or relieve. God grant it may be in my power soon to come to her aid. Our little island continues quite healthy. Yellow fever and cholera are reported prevailing at Key West about sixty miles distant; precautions have been taken to prevent its introduction here.
Your loving husband,
SAM

Little did any of us realize that the prison was sitting on a powder keg…and the fuse was burning intensely.

23

The early sky lightens behind streaks of pink and orange as I watch clouds, lit from underneath, shimmer in a fiery glow. Sunrise intensifies with each minute and draws the world into focus as night falls away. Reflective surfaces of the water take on the color of the sky, like a mirror of light. Shadows dissolve. This is indeed a beautiful place—this prison island, my incarcerated home.

Today I arose early to sweep down the prison walls. I am usually left alone until roll call; this is the only time of day I can enjoy privacy. Often I walk the seawall around the moat, which is almost a mile. The atmosphere is so clear that the space between the sky and the earth seems interminable. Here I can unearth moments of peace, and I feel blessed.

As of late I have felt healthier and noticed that I have gained a little weight, even from this poor food. I reflected that we had not seen the yellow fever here, thank God, yet I am aware that more mosquitoes, fleas and bedbugs infest the island.

In the rainy season our cell floors fill with water after every storm, forcing us to bail them out. We gouged a series of small trenches into the floor leading to a hole so we can scoop the water up and throw it outside every day. Yesterday I bailed twelve bucket loads in less than fifteen minutes. I am concerned that even a little bit of stagnant water can increase the danger of pestilent mosquitoes, roaches and scorpions.

Our drinking water, when we have it, is caught during the rainy season in large reservoirs. Of course there is no ice on the island so we keep our drinking water in porous jars called "monkeys," which we hang in the shade.

We have discovered that during the rainy season hurricanes are a constant threat. We also have "northers" that scurry over the gulf and last three or four days. The thunder echoes and reverberates through the arches and it seems as if the Fort will tumble down about our heads. The trees and coconut branches shake and whimper, and the deep blue water is covered with angry waves. The soldiers sometimes build a fire in our eating room if the temperatures drop. We hear the wind blowing the sand against the windows and comment, "Doesn't that sound like snow?" Then, abruptly, the weather returns to summer temperatures.

Last year, on October 22nd, just four days after we were sent to the dungeon, a terrible hurricane struck the Dry Tortugas. Trees were uprooted, the cattle pen in the parade ground collapsed and the cattle scattered in fear. The howling winds kept us awake all night; just before dawn, the winds blew out the upper story of the officers' quarters. Lieutenant John W. Stirling was killed in his bed and Captain R.A. Stearns was injured. The walls and roofs of many other buildings were brutally damaged. Only the dungeon remained untouched.

At the height of that hurricane, Ned shouted to us above the roar of the winds: "Now if this gets just a bit stronger, perhaps it will lift the island like a raft and carry us to Florida for a holiday!"

"And what would you do once we're ashore?" Colonel Grenfel teased him.

"I am not sure what people do there, but I'd spend a day walking up and down the beach and maybe find a jungle stream for a long cool drink," he replied.

Summer temperatures have been hovering in the 90s and sometimes pass 100 degrees. Coupled with the high humidity, it makes us feel like Maryland crabs in a steamer. Some winter days were almost summer-like, but had cooler breezes. Summer here means stifling air, high humidity, mosquitoes, fleas and bedbugs.

Daily prison life follows the monotonous pattern of any busy army post. In the morning a bugle calls us to rise and shine, assemble for morning roll call and force down our breakfast. The morning gun is fired as the flag is raised over the Fort. Lunch, supper and other events are similarly announced by bugle calls.

In the evening the bugle signals retreat, evening roll call and finally bedtime taps. The evening gun is fired as the flag is lowered for the night. And, when we fall into bed exhausted, we might be awakened by the Fort sentries' loud shouting of the changing of the guard.

My friend Father O'Hara came to see us a few days ago to say goodbye.

"Samuel," he said, "I am being called away by the Bishop."

My face fell. "Father, I am most unhappy to hear that.

Your visits have meant a great deal to my sanity." Immediately I regretted my selfish statement.

"And I have more disarming news," he added. "As far as I can see, there will be no minister or priest here until November."

How will I manage without my confessor, I thought grimly.

Father O'Hara reached into his robe and pulled out a letter. "Perhaps this will cheer you," he smiled. "Your wife managed to send this letter through me, and she even enclosed some money."

I quickly read through it as he waited. When I looked up, his eyes were warm.

"Thank you, Father. I am most grateful to receive some encouraging news. Frank and my children will have help maintaining the farm in my absence. Jere will oversee farm operations and my father and his workers will keep a close eye to make sure everything is running smoothly."

It was gratifying to know that my family was being provided for.

My final confession and communion with Father O'Hara would remain in my heart for a long time. He gently reminded me that I had the means to continue with my daily devotions and prayers.

* * *

I have asked my family not to write anything about the subject of my release, because instead of lessening the bitterness of my banishment and close confinement, it increased it. I explained that I should sooner see it than hear talk of it.

Just recently, I was "officially" assigned to the carpenter's shop at the prison. This is a tremendous improvement in my work detail and has helped lift my morale, mostly because I am learning new skills. I have time to practice the art of cabinet making and have picked up skills to build beautiful pieces, such as an inlaid center table and wreaths and flowers made of collected shells. Ned is showing me how to create a cribbage board, after which I will try my handiness at making a cane. Even before I was assigned to this duty, I spent a good deal of my free time with Ned learning his trade, and have discovered I not only have a small talent for it, but I also enjoy it very much.

Sometimes Grenfel would stop by to chat about ways to decorate the canes Ned and I were carving.

"George, were you ever injured during your time with General Morgan?" Ned Spangler had a passionate interest in Grenfel's role in the Civil War.

Grenfel lifted his brows in surprise. "How did you know?"

"Tell us about it," I added, anxious for another story. Grenfel often relieved our daily routines with his battle stories.

"Hmm, let me think. Well now, it was during the last enemy stronghold, in Cynthiana, Kentucky. I was racing with the leaders of Company C, my scarlet skull cap a-bobbin' as I sprinted to overrun the Federal positions." His eyes were dancing.

"They had a name for me, you know. They called me 'Old St. Lege.' Even the men who disliked me for being a rigid disciplinarian recognized my bravery. I once heard them talking about me, claiming I was the terror of all absentees, stragglers, and deserters. Hah! I am quite fond of that one indeed!"

"And what about your injuries?" prodded Ned.

"In the second charge that day, eleven Yankee bullets pierced my clothing, my cap and also my skin. But I couldn't stop because we were winning. Later, they brought the medic over and he just patched up the wounds."

"How many months were you with Morgan after that?"

"Eight months total, until I finally got fed up with them. I even dropped my efforts to apply British Army discipline to those wild Kentuckians. I declare, I had never encountered such men who would fight like the devil, but then do as they pleased." He laughed, obviously amused. "Those damned Rebel cavalrymen!"

I have mentioned we have no fresh water on the Dry Tortugas, but large cisterns were built into the Fort's foundation to catch and store rainwater. The Fort also has steam condensers for converting sea water into fresh water. Many times these did not work and we had to drink whatever water we could find, or go without.

During these summer months our diet improved slightly, due to fresh fruits arriving on the ships from Cuba. Of course they were expensive, so unless we had extra money, we relied on the generosity of our friends. George Grenfel always had funds and was very generous about sharing fruit with us when the ships arrived with watermelons, pineapples, grapes and bananas. Canned tomatoes and beans were also available infrequently. The large sea turtles were occasionally caught by the soldiers and added variety to our soups and rice and bean dishes.

Although I've not written home about this, we do have a sort of entertainment here. The officers and civilians at the Fort occasionally organized plays for everyone's entertainment, including the prisoners. I will give you the description that one of the soldiers, Alfred O'Donoghue, wrote in a letter to his family.

...a very good theater, gotten up entirely, at very great cost and labor and well supported by the present battalion. There are performances nearly every week. The plays are sent on from New York, and the dramatic company is kept pretty well informed in theatrical matters. The great difficulty that the managers labor under here is the want of female characters, personated by real women. Soldiers do not, as a rule, make good lady characters, and especially here, the face of every man being so well known, their employment in the female department destroys the illusion of reality so necessary to good playing. A shout of derisive laughter often greets the false woman in expansive crinoline; the awkwardness of the figure and long stride betray the deception.

For a brief period we had indeed a real live woman character; the very pretty and talented wife of a non-commissioned officer, since promoted to another department, consented to act with the boys. Her acting and deployment were both excellent, and the enthusiasm on such occasions among the audience was unbounded. On the evening previous to her departure a benefit was given her, and a goodly pile of greenbacks raked in.

George Grenfel and I disagreed about the "very good theater."

"Why, in God's name, do you assist them in their farces?" he questioned.

I smiled. "Because I like the music, and I like to play the fiddle."

"They are so drunk and rowdy yet you give them dancing music to enjoy. I would give them nothing that pleases them," he snorted.

"This is for us, not them. Look at how many of the prisoners look forward to our performances. Some others have even joined our small orchestra, and the soldiers allow us time from work to practice," I grinned. "I am quietly beating them at their own game."

With an abrupt snicker he slapped me on the back and strolled away.

I wonder why I have never shared this part of my prison life with my family. Shame? Self-consciousness? Discretion? I'm not certain why.

24

December 30, 1866

The boats have been coming here less frequently to prevent the spread of the yellow fever and other diseases from the mainland. I am in a bad mood, very impatient for mail and news of my family. My personal mail is inspected by the Fort's military censor, so it can take a month for letters with encouraging reports about my release prospects to arrive. So we must look for clues about the current political climate in newspapers.

Fort Jefferson has a small library with over 250 books and several newspapers, such as the *New York Herald,* the *Washington Chronicle,* and the *London Illustrated News.* Isolated as we are, we consider ourselves fortunate to have access to world news.

On November 31st I wrote another letter to my brother-in-law Jere.

My dear Jere:
Colonel Grenfel handed me a letter he received from A.J. Peeler, a lawyer in Tallahassee, Florida, who intends acting on his case immediately. It seems to me, if you have to resort to law for my release, this would be the least expensive and most expeditious medium. He has

promised to act for the Colonel free of charge, requiring
only the actual expense attendant. With a small amount
from each of us interested parties to pay for trouble, etc.,
he would be pleased to undertake our case. If you con-
clude to act through him, you can address A.J. Peeler's
law office in the South Western Railroad Bank Build-
ing, Tallahassee, Florida. Remember me to all kind
friends and inquirers.
Your brother, etc,
SAM

Everything we learned reduced our now fading hopes for a speedy release. Like a child once enthralled by bright anticipation, I now felt thrown into sudden depths of despondency. Early that November I wrote Frank about my gloomy sense of impatience.

No investigation is being made in regard to my case,
where even the evidence itself against me bears the
impress of untruth without any other refutation. I feel
that I am an American citizen and entitled to the protec-
tion which the Constitution and laws guarantee.

On top of this, I have become very apprehensive about the yellow fever spreading across the Southern states in recent years—with thousands dying in Virginia before the war. Most of us now wear flannel shirts even on the hottest days, to avoid being eaten alive by the insects. I fully suspect the mosquitoes that infest our stagnant water of carrying this dreaded disease.

The prison doctor Brevet Major Joseph Sim Smith and

I have discussed several theories, the most common one being that bad air or "miasmas" bring on the high fever and delirium; bleeding from eyes, nose and ears; digested blood that comes up as "black vomit;" and the jaundice that gives the fever its name. Neither of us has seen or treated patients with the yellow fever, so we have no personal experience. But I fear the mosquitoes could be the root cause for spreading it.

Small packages from home, containing food and other items, are now allowed and I joyfully opened one two days ago. Frankie had sent me some clothing, canned fruit and vegetables, tobacco and whiskey, according to her enclosed note. However, the whiskey had mysteriously disappeared before I received the package.

Prisoners have established a form of bartering and became good at it. The prison gives us a credit of three dollars per month to use at the sutler store, operated just outside the Fort's walls by civilian contractors. We combine our pennies to enjoy various everyday items such as writing paper, pencils, ink, mirrors, pocket knives, toothbrushes, and sometimes even canned food, sweet biscuits and candies. Even whiskey is available for an especially high price. I do not indulge, but George Grenfel enjoys a libation or two from time to time.

We are permitted to build small boxes adorned with sea shells and other similar items to sell to each other and to the soldiers, which brings a little extra money. Our families can send us small monetary amounts as well, so we feel less deprived than we did in the beginning. Ned Spangler was the first to ask if we could do odd jobs around the fort for additional gratuities and "trafficked" items received from home to soldiers, which improved the variety of our amenities.

Those of us who created personal Christmas gifts were anxious to send them in early December. I sent Frank two large moss-cards, a cross and a wreath, enclosed in a letter sent on December 7th.

My darling Frank,
These gifts were pressed by myself. I devote a great deal of my leisure to pressing moss for the want of a more suitable employment, which acts as a diversion to my thoughts, a pastime and a profit. Tell little Tommy that Papa sent him one to pay for the rosebud received some time ago. I had to cut the paper to make it small enough for the envelope. Should these arrive in good condition, and you desire more, let me know, and I will send you more by the same means.

Bear up bravely against present adversity, and I am in hopes it will not be long before we are restored to each other by a merciful Providence. I have not much hope of its taking place during the session of Congress. The time for action was permitted to go by.
Your loving husband,
SAM

During that time, Frank received a letter from R.T. Merrick regarding my case.

Washington, December 17, 1866
My dear Mrs. Mudd:
The Supreme Court of the United States this morning

gave an opinion which must secure the liberation of your husband. I have before spoken to you of the case, and the opinion should have been delivered last winter when the case was decided, but was deferred until the present session. I have been unwilling at any time to say anything to you that might induce hopes, which, if dis-appointed, would only increase your suffering; and pre-ferred to wait until I could myself see the light before I told you there was light, and I am now most happy that I can say to you that I think the case is settled, and your husband must be speedily released from his most unjust confinement.

Deeply sympathizing with you in your long suffering, and congratulating you sincerely upon the prospect of its termination, I remain, with great respect,
Yours truly,
R.T. Merrick

Of course, I did not get any such information for another month; by then, the "light" he mentioned seemed to have dimmed once again.

It was not to be. Christmas passed without any hopes to distract us from disagreeable reflection of our situation and regrets for past mistakes. I can only turn to idyllic scenes of my past to muster up a nostalgic smile at the little oddities and sayings of my wife and our dear little ones, then all too soon must return to the current depressing reality.

25

Major Valentine Stone arrived at Fort Jefferson on April 25th to assume command. His first act was to send former commander Lieutenant Robinson (the officer who had ordered George Grenfel chained and thrown into the water three times) to Key West where he would face charges of prisoner and soldier abuse.

With his typical aplomb, Grenfel quickly befriended Major Stone and now enjoyed a marked improvement in personal comfort.

"He asked me where I wanted to work," he stated, his eyes twinkling. "I answered that I might enjoy returning to garden work."

At the beginning of the year, some of us were given permission to plant a small garden in the center of the Fort, using rich soil supplied from the mainland. It was now luxuriant with beets, peas, tomatoes, beans, radishes, and strawberries; everything grew well in that black soil. We also enjoyed a variety of flowers in bloom and one or two little caged songbirds to enliven the island with sporadic merry notes. Grenfel was especially fond of the birds.

"And can you believe this?" he teased, his face wreathed in smiles. "I've just received a parcel from Jefferson

Davis." Smiling broadly, he thrust the packet at me containing a letter, some tobacco and twenty dollars.

"This communication will do wonders for your spirit," I told him after reading the letter. "It is exactly what your doctor would prescribe."

In the letter Jefferson Davis conveyed his sympathy and told him the Florida legislature was being pressured to release the former Confederate President from Fortress Monroe without delay or rancor. He encouraged Grenfel to become more hopeful as well.

Smiling into his beard like a satiated wolf, Grenfel invited me to accompany him to the moat and celebrate along with his pet Hawksbill sea turtle.

We sat on the beach, outside the Fort's forbidding presence, and almost forgot that we were there against our will. The beach was smooth, like shiny ice, and the water was so still and silent. The water barely moved in and out. We appreciated the silence of that spot.

Grenfel had turned one corner of the most secluded section into Liberty's private habitat. Almost a year ago he found Liberty, a young turtle stranded on a shard of coral reef. He realized that its flipper was injured so he picked him up, cleaned out the wound and nursed him back to health. Then he decided to adopt him as a pet and named him Liberty.

I laughed as Liberty lifted up his head and shuffled forth from under some sea grass when he heard Grenfel calling out his name.

"I remember when you tethered him for quite some time while treating him, because you were so worried he might wander off into dangerous waters," I said with half a smile.

"Indeed, but that was before I realized he was not only intelligent but possessed a great sense of humor," he chuckled, watching the turtle lumber along the sand on tip-toe, his head and neck stretched out eagerly toward Grenfel.

"Liberty loves his treats, and comes running for something special! Oh my gallant boy, today we shall dine on lettuce from the garden as well as strawberries and grapes fresh from the sutler's store!"

Grenfel squatted regally beside the turtle to watch him feast. His pet's beautiful colored shell of thick, overlapping scales gleamed in the sunlight and reminded me of why tortoise shell decorations were in such demand.

Liberty's powerful hawk-like beak grabbed at the grapes and juice was soon running down his chin. When Grenfel held out a large strawberry, Liberty became positively hysterical, lumbering to and fro, gazing at him pleadingly with his tiny button eyes. Finally able to snatch the berry, he held it firmly while stumbling off at top speed to his safe and secluded nest where he could drop the fruit and eat at his leisure.

Liberty also developed a craving for human company, especially Grenfel's. However, when any of us came into his area to sit, which we occasionally did, it wasn't long before Liberty's craggy and earnest face would poke through the sea grass. He contented himself with getting as close to our feet as possible, and then sinking into a deep and peaceful sleep, his head drooping out of his shell, his nose resting on the sand, with an expression of bemused good humor on his face.

Liberty now measured about 30 centimeters, and would

one day reach his adult weight of 150 to 200 pounds. I speculated about what would happen to him if we left the island, as he was so accustomed to humans. I wondered if Grenfel would take him with him.

The number of prisoners at the Fort was down to about forty-five, including both black and white. A rumor was spreading that we might all be taken to Ship Island in Mississippi. Major Stone told us that it was located sixty miles from New Orleans and ninety miles from Fort Pickens, and that there was a fort situated on the western end of the island.

I had recently received an interesting piece of mail. My attorney sent me a copy of John Wilke Booth's diary, found in a pocket of his clothing at the time of his death, which was withheld from the Court that had convicted us. We who are languishing in prison here see no reason for this, nor do we understand the motives. It clearly confirms the statement of all those who participated with him, or who were Confederates. It shows unmistakably that I could have had no knowledge of the deed, and it would have established my innocence. I will send all this information to Frankie and let her and the family deal with it, agreeable to their best judgment.

Ruminating on my feelings today, our country seems to be a complete "monocracy" instead of a government of law and order. Our President does not feel warranted to execute his duties under the Constitution without first consulting the mob spirit. I grow exceedingly weary of the continued usurpation. If I felt the government had the slightest shadow of suspicions against me, I might feel more resigned; but considering the entirety of evidence and circumstances presented at trial, no court of justice could fail to establish my total innocence. I said this to Judge Turner on my way to this prison and he answered me with: "Well, someone has to suffer, and it was just as well that you should as anybody else." I appreciated his answer, but could never see the justice.

Jefferson Davis has now been set free. Surratt, who was extradited from Egypt last year and sent to trial, was once regarded as Davis's prime agent. Now it seems that most, if not all, the charges against him have been removed. Here I am, having suffered the tortures of the damned, without a word of rebuke to those who have caused it all—and without pity, sympathy, or consolation from an enlightened public.

We have had several days of continuous storms, with intense dampness which penetrates every joint and brings up every old rheumatic disposition. To obviate the evil effects of the dampness I am forced to constantly wear flannel or net shirts. I believe this helps against the mosquitos and other creatures that molest our exposed limbs.

I have just sat down to write Frank and the children. I will tell them my health continues to be good, and that I feel depressed only occasionally. I feel this is partly due to our new commander and his kindness to the few prisoners who remain. And of course Grenfel is much happier, and continues to entertain us with his outrageous stories.

Reading the newspaper only tends to engender hate and makes my mind dwell on crimes of every description. For the time being, I am ignoring them. I long for just an afternoon with my family, and will remind Frank to train our sweet children to obedience and good behavior now while they are still young, in order to spare them the blush of shame for unruly conduct when they grow older.

When I contemplate my family, I feel peace of mind. And that I seek above all else.

26

September 8, 1867

No one is certain exactly when the yellow fever reached the Dry Tortugas. Some say Company K's Captain George W. Crabbe brought it with him from Cuba on August 17th, which was the day before his first symptoms appeared. Two days later a second Company K soldier was felled with the disease.

At the time four hundred people were living in the Fort, including forty-five prisoners.

On August 22nd, Private James Forsythe, 5th U.S. Artillery, was the first to die. Private Joseph Enits died next, on August 30th. The fever has now spread to Company L and to the officers' servants.

I was still working at the carpentry shop but immediately set out to speak with the prison doctor, Dr. Joseph Sim Smith. He was a Union surgeon and had been a classmate of mine at Georgetown College. I offered him my assistance.

"Quite a panic exists among soldiers and officers," I told him. "I am willing to do whatever you need."

He readily agreed, so we discussed treatment of the symptoms.

"They say Tiger mosquitoes entered on the persons

and luggage of some Company K soldiers," he told me. "Neither you nor I has ever seen a case of the yellow fever, yet we must quickly come up with a treatment."

"Should we consider removing the healthy children from their sick parents?" I wondered aloud.

Dr. Smith nodded. "I see the wisdom in that strategy."

By September 3rd, three more cases of the fever had proven fatal. We then decided to erect a makeshift quarantine hospital on Sand Key, a tiny island two and a half miles away. Two companies were quickly shipped to other keys to keep them from the contagion, and two remained to guard the inmates.

I worked day and night to help Dr. Sim Smith, and when he contracted the disease on September 5th, along with his wife, I was devastated. Fortunately the children did not show any symptoms and were quickly quarantined.

Major Valentine Stone came to me the day Dr. Smith fell ill, clearly agitated and frightened.

"Please, Dr. Mudd, carry on the best you can until a replacement for Dr. Smith arrives." I assured him I would, despite the shock of suddenly finding myself in this ominous position. It would require struggling with contending emotions of fear and responsibility.

I barely saw my friends Spangler, Arnold, or O'Laughlen, but Grenfel came to visit me when he could.

"Anything I can do, ol' chap?" he would ask with his lopsided grin.

"You can make me laugh, if possible," I answered, weary and irritable. "I sometimes wonder why I am working myself to death to save those who hold my fate in their hands."

"Now, hear me out. The yellow fever is the most fair and square thing I have seen in the past few years. It makes no distinction in regard to rank, color, or previous condition—every man has his chance. I would advise you as a friend not to interfere."

My exhaustion overwhelmed me and I struggled against the bitterness. I have been deprived of liberty, banished from home, family and friends, bound in chains for having exercised a simple act of common humanity in setting the leg of a man for whose insane act I had no sympathy, but which was in line with my professional calling. It is but natural that resentment and fear should rankle in my heart.

Grenfel draped his long arm across my shoulder. "Yet now ye have thrown yourself into providing patients' care."

Looking up at him from a patient's bed, I smiled lethargically. "Do ye good for evil. That's what you are telling me, correct?"

He nodded, handing me clean towels. "Aye, that alone distinguishes the man from the brute."

I had learned that Grenfel said as much with his hands and eyes and the motions of his head as he did with words, which he chose carefully.

I spoke with the commanding officer about terminating the arrangement of sending away the sick in open boats over rough seas. He agreed, and together we decided to send as many of the well soldiers as could be spared from the garrison to other islands, so we could care for the sick here at the Fort.

Patients were being treated in the Post Hospital within

the Fort and at Sand Key Hospital on an adjacent island. This hospital filled quickly as the fever became epidemic. The fever was raging through the ranks of Company K, and had spread to Company L, Company I and to the prisoners' quarters. Isolating it was no longer possible; we could only try to save as many patients as we could.

Our medical treatment was to induce purging and sweating to treat the fevers, and we also administered calomel, a mercury-based drug that caused vomiting, followed up with a dose of Dover's powder, which contained ipecac and opium to encourage sweating.

I visited Dr. Sim Smith this morning. He wanted to guzzle cold water to abate his fever.

"Doctor, you know I cannot allow you to do that, but here is some warm herbal tea," I offered the fevered man.

"It won't be long now," he moaned. "Allow Grenfel to be your head nurse; he's practically doing that already."

I reassured him that his wife was slowly recovering, and that the children had been isolated with their nanny. He drifted back into an agitated sleep.

This afternoon Grenfel and I worked at a feverish pace. When I visited Dr. Sim Smith's children, his three-year-old son had contracted the fever. So far only the seven-year-old daughter remained healthy. My heart went out to them; then ached for my own children.

At dinner time I was called into Dr. Sim Smith's quarters. His ill wife and I sat with him as he succumbed to the yellow fever. I could not hold back my tears, but promised them both to save his children.

That was a promise I would not keep.

27

OCTOBER 16, 1867

By October 1st our situation was becoming desperate. My hopes surged upon the arrival of reinforcements in the form of Dr. D. W. Whitehurst, an elderly surgeon from Key West. I hoped that together we could uncover the root cause of the disease and stop its spread. We had learned how to treat the symptoms, but not what was triggering the horrible disease.

Since Dr. Sim Smith's demise, I was the island's only doctor, so it was more important than ever to make changes if the disease's spread was to be slowed. I implemented several hygienic practices that I believed would save lives.

First, I gave orders to discontinue the practice of placing a new patient in the same bed as a recently deceased one. Then I closed down the Sand Key quarantine and treated those patients at the main hospital, reasoning that isolation would ensure their deaths without stopping the fever's spread. I also instituted a new policy to use only clean bedding and clothes on sick beds. And it worked!

I wrote to Frank about Dr. Smith's son: *He is a very intelligent child, and has amused me on several occasions. I fear he will not get over the yellow fever ... A little daughter about seven years old remains exempt, having been sent to a different portion of the Fort. The little boy was very fond of me, and used to turn somersaults for me.*

A day later I added: *I visited my little pet today, and found him, to my great sorrow, almost in the agonies of death.* And on September 18, I wrote her this: *The little son of Mrs. Smith died at 3 o'clock this morning; poor woman, she has lost her husband and son—not being here more than six weeks. Their little girl survives; she will leave by the first boat to the North.*

I couldn't bear to tell her that my dear young friend had literally died in my arms.

Sam Arnold wrote to his family, sharing part of his letter with me. *The fever raged in our midst, creating havoc among those dwelling there. Dr. Mudd was never idle. He worked both day and night, and was always at post, faithful to his calling.*

His kind words humbled me, while accurately describing the nightmare of those traumatic days.

Dr. Whitehurst and I suspected that the victims were passing the infection along to one another through a mysterious process called "miasma": a poisonous vapor with suspended particles of decaying and foul-smelling matter. We thought it could be spread by the mosquito.

The yellow fever could be extremely painful. It usually started with a severe headache, after which the pain traveled down the spine until it hit the back of the legs. This illness was also called "bone fever." Just when it seemed to be clearing up and the patient thought he was cured, it returned—much worse than before. It brought with it chills, fever, and almost unbearable thirst. In its final stages, it turned the victim's skin yellow.

For those who did not die recovery was rapid, and they were back at work in ten days or so. But during their time in hospital, the patients required almost constant attention by Grenfel, his assistant nurses and both of us—the two Fort doctors. Many of my letters home had to be written late at night, after my final round of the wards and right before my quick nap. I re-read one written just over one month ago, still grieving the losses.

My darling Frank,
Today, September 13, 1867, we have scarcely well ones enough to attend the sick and bury the dead. They are not suffered to grow cold before they are hurried off to the grave. Dr. Whitehurst, from Key West and the original doctor who was expelled from the island in the beginning of the war, (on account of the sympathies of his wife), is now an incessant laborer. He is quite an old man, but has endeared himself to all by his Christian, constant, and unremitting attention at all hours, even when duty seemed not to require. I remain up every night until twelve or later. He is up the balance of the night, and there never was greater accord of medical opinion. I have been restored to liberty of the island at all hours, day or night, but have time only to serve the sick. Every officer is down with the disease, and but one remains to perform all the duties. He is a newcomer from Baltimore, recently married, whose name is Lieutenant Gordon.

This disease ends its course quickly, but has to be treated in time to get the patient through the first stage in order that a successful termination may be promised.

I have resigned myself to the fates, and shall no more
act upon my own impulse. Not one of the prisoners has
as yet died, and those that take the disease pass through it
without any apparent suffering.

Learning that Sam Arnold and Michael O'Laughlen had
fallen ill was the last straw: I broke down in unbearable
despair, my heart exploding in sorrow as I comforted my
close friend Michael during his convulsion—terrified he
was dying in front of me.

Grenfel held me in his arms and tried to console me as
I covered my face with my handkerchief, wracked with
sobs.

"We will save them, Doc," he whispered. "Together,
we can do it. And perhaps a little prayer would come in
handy." Even then, he brought a smile to my face. We
prayed together.

Quite suddenly, Lieutenant Gordon became ill with
the fever and was carried out to be buried eleven days
later. On September 21st, the wife of the post commander
Major Stone died suddenly, and he left immediately by
ship to get his two-year-old son out of danger. The child
was saved, but Major Stone had developed the disease
here at Fort Jefferson and died in Key West, just four
days after his wife passed.

Having spent so much time in that prison, I recognized every inch and corner of every room. Despite all
those bad memories and reminders of past travail, I had
never understood how malevolent and dangerous a room
can begin to feel; once familiar walls seemed to swell and
threatened to smother me.

My eyes felt raw from weeping, every moment a Hell with no apparent escape route. I learned to will parts of my consciousness dead and cold and calm, and became proficient enough so that parts of each day were spent out of pain's crushing path.

I had seen so much death, held a child as he died and gripped the hands of others as they breathed their last.

This uniquely helpless sense of failure is one that every doctor must accept with his diploma. But no amount of experience or understanding can prepare us to deal reasonably with such unremitting tragedy.

Clutching a dear friend to my breast as he passed away was emotionally unbearable. Samuel Arnold recovered; Michael O'Laughlen succumbed despite our constant attention.

I nursed him through his final moments on September 23rd, desperately applying cold rags to his face and body as his light began to fade.

"Doctor, Doctor, you must tell my mother all," he cried out. His voice cracked and tears ran down his cheeks. I held him and told him I loved him. He was still conscious and could still talk, but he knew he was done.

Then he called Ned Spangler over and said, "Goodbye, Ned."

There was no time for farewells. The moment someone passed, and sometimes just before he died, a plain wooden box was brought alongside his bed so that the infected body could be removed from the hospital as rapidly as possible. Less than thirty minutes after the death was certified, the burial party moved in.

The body was placed in the waiting coffin, the lid was

nailed shut and the coffin was carried to a boat, rowed a mile to another island and lowered into a previously dug hole. No one wanted the duty to carry and bury the deceased. There was fear that whoever picked up the dead body or touched the blanket he was wrapped in might get the fever himself. The men who did this were given liberal doses of whiskey, but this didn't make the work any easier or safer.

Just when I thought nothing more terrible could happen to us, Colonel George Grenfel's exhaustion caught up with him. The old soldier, tired and weak from loss of sleep, collapsed and had to be put in bed alongside his dying patients. He had worked so hard as their chief nurse, and now, because of his advanced age, he had little strength remaining to fight the deadly yellow fever.

"Fight, my Colonel," I implored him, tears dripping down my face. "We need you here. Don't leave me! I will do all that is possible to save you."

"Doc, I shan't leave you," he wheezed. "I have lived through wars with the Arabs, South and North Americans, Indians and Russians. It won't be easy for this blasted disease to finish me!"

My prayers were answered. He lived.

I, on the other hand, almost didn't. While caring for Grenfel and scarcely sleeping, I came down with the splitting headache and the back pains. I told no one. When the chills and fever hit me, the others knew. It was October 4th, forty-seven days after the beginning of the epidemic.

Two volunteer nurses moved in to watch over me twenty-four hours a day. I was unaware of how they bathed me in cool water and wrapped my chilled body in blankets. Mopping my brow as the sweat poured off, they dug into my medicine chest for the drugs they knew I had given to the other patients. When I was semi-conscious, I saw through a haze how they ate and slept in shifts, never leaving me alone. When I finally woke up and the fever had passed, I recognized my nursing angels: Samuel Arnold and Ned Spangler, my "co-conspirators" and best friends.

"Our hero has returned to us," murmured Arnold.

"Praise God," acclaimed Spangler, wrapping me in a gentle embrace.

I looked behind him and saw Grenfel, his cheeks wet with tears.

"I think this is one of my happiest moments," I muttered. "My guardian angels have brought me back." I later learned I owed my life to the unremitting care that Arnold and Spangler, and their nurse Grenfel, had bestowed on me.

28

OCTOBER 28, 1867

On October 14th, the day I recovered, I was told the worst of the epidemic was over. It had left a terrible toll. Of the approximately three hundred fifty people at Fort Jefferson, including soldiers, civilians, and prisoners, some two hundred seventy had been struck down by the yellow fever. Thirty-eight died. I could never understand why the soldiers had suffered worse than the prisoners and the whites more severely than the blacks.

By the end of October, the yellow fever epidemic had abated and we had no new cases except for the new Army physician, Dr. Edward Thomas. All the other patients were convalescing. Although not fully recovered, I took over Dr. Thomas's cases and administered to all those who were still ill. Many of the Fort's occupants were still showing signs of the fever's lingering symptoms as they stumbled down the path toward recovery. Remarkably, my friend Ned Spangler was one of the few at Fort Jefferson who had not fallen ill.

As with any group of people who have lived through a disaster together, the survivors shared a strong sense of camaraderie. This was especially noticeable with Arnold and Spangler, who repeatedly mentioned the special tie they felt with me, whose life they had saved.

"I am so indebted to both of you and Grenfel," I told them. The lump in my throat was so huge I could barely swallow. "You three kept me alive." My voice sounded like a whisper.

Spangler, who had become my cellmate during the epidemic, had made sure I wasn't distracted while struggling to nurse the sick back to health, and that I had time for short rest breaks. He also enjoyed entertaining everyone with a steady stream of jokes.

Even the soldiers, who had originally despised the four Lincoln conspirators, found it impossible not to laugh whenever this shabby, uneducated, unshaven carpenter demonstrated his droll sense of humor.

Once, standing in the yard, he thoughtfully began studying the roof of the Fort and stroking his chin. Directly in front of him stood a normally unfriendly sergeant.

"D'ye know, Sir, if you'll find me the lumber and nails I could build ye a private room on the roof," he murmured, as if to himself. "Then, ye could get more sea breezes!"

Sergeant O'Connor turned away slightly to attempt to hide the laughter now rumbling up from his chest. When that didn't work he turned the guffaw into a cough and strode away officiously.

After the yellow fever epidemic subsided and because I took on Dr. Sim Smith's duties, my status in the prison again changed dramatically: no more locked cells, no more chains, and no more cleaning bricks. I had the run of the Fort and enjoyed the heady experience of being respected by the enlisted men and treated as a gentleman by the officers.

Led by one grateful survivor, Lieutenant Edmund L. Zalinski, they wrote a petition to President Johnson asking that I be released from prison and returned to my family. This document, signed by the full complement of two hundred and ninety-nine officers and soldiers, stated that my medical skills, courage and unselfishness had saved countless lives and prevented a dangerous panic in the fort. It ended with the following words: *Many here, who have experienced his kind and judicious treatment, can never repay him the debt of obligation they owe him.*

Major Stone promised to personally present my case to General Grant once he returned to Washington. He left with his young child, but then died only days later in Key West. The message died with him. A month later, as with many petitions for pardon, mine completely vanished inside the War Department files.

* * *

I sent my wife a copy of this formal petition to the government, explaining to her how it was written and signed without my knowledge. I asked her and Jere to review it, and if they considered it beneficial to my case, to make the decision whether to present it in person to the President.

The petition I sent to Frank was signed only by the non-commissioned officers; the other copy, designed for the President, had been signed by every officer and soldier in the garrison. Below is the one I included in her letter of October 22, 1867.

Copy of the Petition at the Dry Tortugas
For the release of Dr. Mudd
(All names of signers omitted)

It is with sincere pleasure that we acknowledge the great services rendered by Dr. S.A. Mudd (prisoner) during the prevalence of yellow fever at the Fort. When the very worthy surgeon of the Post, Dr. J. Sim Smith, fell one of the first victims of the fatal epidemic, and the greatest dismay and alarm naturally prevailed on all sides, deprived as the garrison was of the assistance of any medical officer, Dr. Mudd, influenced by the most praiseworthy and humane motives, spontaneously and unsolicited came forward to devote all his energies and professional knowledge to the aid of the sick and dying.

He inspired the hopeless with courage, and by his constant presence in the midst of danger and infection, regardless of his own life, tranquillized the fearful and desponding. By his prudence and foresight, the hospital upon an adjacent island, to which at first the sick were removed in an open boat, was discontinued. Those attacked with the malady were on the spot put under vigorous treatment. A protracted exposure on the open sea was avoided, and many now strong doubtless owe their lives to the care and treatment they received at his hands.

He properly considered the nature and character of the infection and concluded that it could not be eradicated by the mere removal of the sick, entailing, as it did, the loss of valuable time necessary for the application of the proper remedies, exposure of those attacked and adding to the general fear and despondency. The entire different system of treatment and hospital arrangement was resorted to with the happiest effect. Dr. Mudd's treatment and the change which he recommended met with the hearty approval and warm commendation of the regularly appointed surgeons, with whom, in a later stage of the epidemic, he was associated. Many here who have experienced his kind and judicious treatment, can never repay him the debt of obligation they owe him. We do, therefore, in consideration of the invaluable services rendered by him during this calamitous and fatal epidemic, earnestly recommend him to the well-merited clemency of the Government, and solicit his immediate release from here, and restoration to liberty and the bosom of his family.

At the letter's end, I explained: *As of today, I have not yet, for reasons best known to myself, presented the instrument to the officers of the Post. The whole garrison have an unbounded confidence in my opinion, and have said they prefer me to the regularly appointed physicians. There seems to be an idea among some, however, that by signing the instrument they might detract from the knowledge and intelligence of my associates in medicine, and thereby cause displeasure.*

Finally, I wrote another letter to Frank and Jere and asked them to inform me plainly about the opinion of the public in regard to the course I should pursue.

We have just been visited by a member of the Butler Congressional Committee to obtain statements in regard to the assassination. I swore under oath (and in writing) that I did not know anything about the matter, or parties concerned, previous to the assassination. But we three who were interviewed here at the Fort have doubts about the

matter, because we believe that Congress has acknowl-
edged the illegality of our imprisonment and trial by ask-
ing and receiving an oath from us. Poor Sam Arnold was
quite sick with dysentery while giving his statement, and
the labor and excitement aggravated the symptoms.

Please mention this fact to counsel and to members of
Congress who may be favorably disposed.

A few nights ago, I dreamed I was with Tommy and
Sammy. The emotion which it produced soon broke my
slumber, and away fled all my happiness; such has been
and continues to be my life, until I almost fear to hope. Try
for the future, my good Frank, not to unsettle my mind
with mere speculations, but tell me frankly and plainly
the whole truth. Let me know all the correct news, and if
anything new has developed in regard to the assassination.
Your devoted husband,
SAM

I eventually learned the real reason for Gleason's trip to
Fort Jefferson. President Johnson had finally found the
nerve to suspend his old nemesis, Secretary of War Stanton. In response, Congress announced its intent to remove
Johnson from office through the impeachment process.
The first vote had supported the President 108 to 57, and
Stanton's friends were getting worried. So they sent Gleason to interview me and the others at Fort Jefferson, hoping for another way to discredit the President.

29

December 15, 1867

The Fort has a new commanding officer, Major George P. Andrews. Not having suffered with us through the epidemic, he hasn't been as favorably disposed towards the prisoners as Commander Stone. When I asked him for an update on my petition to the President, he said he had no idea what I was talking about. Naturally, I could no longer trust him.

As usual I found Grenfel by the water. He was reading aloud to Liberty the sea turtle, who appeared to be asleep, his head drooping out of his shell. Liberty roused himself to greet me, lifting his heavy eyes and chirping softly. I acknowledged his greeting by gently stroking his scaly head.

"I say ol' man, to what do we owe this visit?" George asked, smiling and unhurriedly closing his book.

"What do you think of Major Andrews?" I asked without preamble.

"The bloke seems like a typical officer." A sigh rumbled through his chest. "What say you?"

"I suspect he doesn't much like us conspirators. He won't look us in the eye, and I know he distrusts us." I sat down beside him. "Does he speak with you?"

He laughed with contempt. "The cheek of him! You

must know that everyone speaks with me; I demand it. If I want an answer, I shall get right up in their faces until I get it."

We laughed, and changed the subject. Liberty returned to his snooze.

It wasn't long before my suspicions were confirmed.

I wrote to Frank on December 7th. I had many disheartened and disappointing bits of news to share with her so I attempted to be as gentle as I could, knowing how much she had prayed for my release and freedom.

> *My dearest Frank:*
> *I received your last, dated November 7, which gave me much comfort. God grant your anticipation may prove correct. Judging from the tone of the papers, I fear there will be great difficulty to contend against. Our country seems now not to be governed by the Constitution, or by law, but by unbridled popular or public opinion, of which I have no doubt many others, as in my case, have been made victims.*
> *I am very well but back in chains, and along with four others, under guard once again. Our duty now is to wash down the bastions of the fort each day. I have gotten used to my present life, and do not feel much incommoded. God grant that I may soon be in the fond embrace of you and our dear little ones.*
> *Good-bye,*
> *SAM*

Several days after mailing that letter, I learned that Frank had been informed personally by the Honorable

Montgomery Blair—Commandant of Fort Jefferson in Washington City—that the petition written by the soldiers had never been received in Washington. I wrote to him immediately, knowing I had nothing to lose.

Were I in other circumstances, modesty would compel me to refrain from the least notoriety, but in my present situation, not only my personal ease and comfort, but the anguish and distress of a wife and four helpless little children, cause me to throw off this humility, and solicit your kind office in my behalf.

I refer you to the hospital report to draw conclusions as to the services rendered here at Fort Jefferson. Upon the sickness and death of Dr. Smith, our lamented surgeon, I was placed in charge of the hospital by Major Stone, who vested me with discretionary power in all that pertains to the duties of a physician. Immediately I discontinued the Sand Key Hospital. I used blankets instead of sheets, and had the hospital windows arranged differently.

At the time, we had twenty cases under active treatment; many delirious. Less than six hours later, under my management, all were free from fever and seemed comfortable. They all recovered. One afterward was taken with relapse and died. I refer you to Colonel Hamilton, who was here at the time, and to the non-commissioned officers of the companies. I was strenuously opposed by Major Stone in the breaking up of the Sand Key Hospital, but finally convinced him that if he left the disposition of the sick to my judgment, I would faithfully consult the greatest good to the greatest number, to which he consented.

I never received a response. I feel strongly that Major Andrews destroyed it before it could even leave the Fort.

The winter had begun unusually mild. Colonel Grenfel described it aptly in a letter to one of his snowbound friends in Indiana: *We inhabitants of Fort Jefferson never need to blow on our fingers to keep warm. As it is, we rarely even have to sleep under a blanket.*

We had all observed changes in our treatment by the prison authorities; certainly not as friendly as the times following the epidemic, yet not as stringent as what we had been subjected to soon after we arrived. Despite inflexible orders from their higher-ups, the guards understood the heavy debt they owed to Grenfel, Spangler, Arnold and myself and tried to make our lives as pleasant as they could. For example, they still allowed me to bring out the fiddle and play occasionally at our gatherings.

I was encouraged to see the renewed interest that Congress was taking in the assassination case. This began with the visit of William H. Gleason to interview the defendants, since we hadn't been allowed to testify under oath at our own trial. Now we were encouraged privately to be sworn in and provide our side of the story.

Arnold later told me that he knew he wasn't *completely innocent,* and feared that anything he said might be used against him in future proceedings.

"I refused to make a statement at first, owing to being so sick, but when they told me I was gonna be put in solitary until I talked, I changed my mind the next day."

"So you were threatened!" Grenfel growled indignantly. "They are still menacing us." The anger surfaced suddenly, seen through a threatening light flashing in his eyes.

When we lined up before Gleason, we realized what he really had in mind. Congress didn't actually care about Arnold or Spangler as such, or even the Booth story. What they wanted was someone to lie under oath and tie President Johnson into Lincoln's assassination.

Once we figured that out, we waited to see what came next. We didn't have to wait long.

"As you know, Mr. Arnold and Mr. Spangler, we do have evidence that you played roles in the assassination."

Neither man flinched. "If you choose to cooperate and lie under oath, you will be freed from Fort Jefferson and taken back to Washington as witnesses."

The room was silent. No one had mentioned my name, so I felt like I would not be offered anything. I had already determined not to become a part of this perjury and bear false witness.

"Take your time and think about it. We will discuss it this afternoon," he told them, walking out of the room.

Arnold and Spangler turned to me. "Do you believe any of this?" asked Ned.

"No, I don't Ned," I answered slowly. "I believe nothing they say." How quickly things could happen, lives turning askew, when one was simply going along.

"'Tis a tempting offer," added Samuel, "but I won't take the chance of giving them the pleasure of believing their lies."

"Nor will I." To their profound credit, Ned and Sam had decided to stand their ground along with me.

That afternoon, Gleason returned, accompanied by Major Andrews. I was not in the room during the cross-examination, but when they told me the story, I was disgusted.

Sam related it concisely and to the point.

We told them we would not lie under oath. Major Andrews immediately told us he would have me shot if I didn't help Gleason.

"Do you understand me, Samuel Arnold? Do I make myself perfectly clear?" There was violence in him, ordered and controlled.

"I do, Sir," I answered, digesting his words.

Again, I refused, and that's when they called in the post surgeon to discuss my case.

Eventually, Gleason came over to where we were standing and told us they would not do that at this time because I was still a sick man.

Throughout all this excitement my lawyers continued to work on their case to free me. As mentioned previously, I had written a letter to Commandant Major Andrews notifying him of my knowledge that my petition, written by the soldiers, had not been received in Washington. As expected, I received no response to my letter. I did welcome a very kind letter from Dr. Whitehurst, thanking me for my noble conduct during his stay on the island, to which I responded gratefully.

I was slowly regaining my peace of mind. Now, all I could do was wait.

30

MARCH 30, 1868

I am truly surprised that none of us saw it coming. Maybe because we "Lincoln conspirators" were once again placed under close guard and given little free time to communicate with each other. Or perhaps because Colonel Grenfel chose to keep his plans close to his heart. In any case, it was a jolt to us all that he was able to pull it off.

Grenfel told me he had given up any satisfaction from the judicial process. As he slowly recovered his general health, he spent as much time as he could building up muscle mass and resilience. With spring on the way, he had been secretly planning his return to England. Major Andrews's offensive dictatorship led him to seek out three other men desperate enough to risk their lives with him on the open seas.

"George, I can see how hard you are working to gain upper body strength," I commented one afternoon. "Are you planning an escape?" It was asked in jest and I expected no answer.

"Well now ol' fellow, you once told me you would never again attempt escape. That assured me I could not count on you for assistance," he said with an acerbic smile. "I just may be forced to try it on my own. Seems the weather should be just right, a boat has to be available and I shall need some sailors to lend a hand."

I tried to study his facial features and sincerity behind his serene expression. This man had taken lives and risked his own. He truly believed in law and order and justice. Just as he believed in the sword.

It wasn't easy to dismiss his idle chatter as simple conversation. Then I remembered a prisoner named Adair who had escaped to Cuba, where he was captured and returned to Fort Jefferson. He and Colonel Grenfel had since become good friends, often sitting together on the beach as they quietly conversed. A few weeks before our conversation, Adair had requested and been given permission to move into Grenfel's cell. Had someone been paid for that favor?

Another prisoner, Joseph Holroyd, slept in the mess hall on the ground floor and could easily assist them in slipping out through a nearby gun opening in the wall. His cellmate was James Orr.

On the night of March 6, 1868, Private William Noreil of the Fifth United States Artillery was on sentry duty at Wharf Number One. Noreil possessed a key to the cell occupied by Grenfel and Adair.

In what would later seem to be a miracle given that night's events, the garrison had been reduced to a bare minimum. Many soldiers had been sent to New Orleans to help quell a disturbance there. My fellow conspirators and I had not even been considered to help back up the remaining soldiers, as we were too "risky."

A gale had been buffeting the Fort for six days. Grenfel

counted on this downpour to keep the guards from seeing more than several feet in front of them. The roar of the wind would prevent them from hearing anything less than a cannon shot. In addition, a Coast Guard cutter had pulled into the Dry Tortugas harbor shortly after dark, seeking shelter from the angry waves.

The timing was perfect. Private Noreil had already agreed to assist the four prisoners in the madcap adventure. He slipped away from his sentry post and freed Grenfel and Adair. The three of them set out with Holroyd to swim past the choppy moat—under driving sheets of angry rain and continuous, lashing streaks of lightning—and meet Orr on the far side. Then the four joined forces and pushed a tiny sailboat out into the huge waves pounding over the breakwaters, succeeding against all odds. If the Coast Guardsmen feared challenging the storm in their much bigger craft, how could these amateurs succeed in a tiny boat?

The Fort's inhabitants learned about the escape just after sunrise by the ringing of the alarm bell. Search parties were quickly dispatched in every direction, but returned soaked to the skin and empty-handed. They had found no debris or floating bodies.

I was devastated with the report. It finally dawned on me how much I cared for Colonel Grenfel. I went down to the beach, looking for Liberty.

He came to me as I called his name. I sat with him, inconsolable, with the rain whipping over the rails, splashing us both.

"He's left you, my friend," I said, as a wave of grief washed over me. "I thought he might take you if he ever tried to escape." Absentmindedly scratching Liberty's head, I carried on. "He's left me as well."

Liberty opened his eyes and looked directly into mine, and that saddened me. I moved closer and knelt in front of his sizable face. "I think he wanted you to be my charge."

Fingering my rosary beads, I allowed the soft blanket of familiar sensations to envelope me. Slowly I began to appreciate this disheartening moment with the solitary beach, Liberty and God. Yet there was no consolation. Something very important had been taken from me.

Leaning back on my elbows, I looked up at the sky. The rain had suddenly abated, leaving behind a clear dawn. I wanted to stay there with Liberty, listening to the waves lapping against the sand.

I could feel the stillness of the morning gliding over me like a cast net.

* * *

All the prisoners felt a deep loss for the men who had escaped. Most of them assumed they had perished at sea, but I did not. Rumors spread among us that they could have survived, under Grenfel's guidance. We believed they could have reached Cuba and later, parts unknown. I knew Grenfel's love of liberty would be stronger than the enormous risks to his life.

I hadn't heard from him, nor did I expect to. He knew I would take care of Liberty. In a letter to Frank, I wrote the following words: *We have heard nothing from Grenfel since he escaped on the 6th of March. All hands may have perished, it being quite stormy at the time.*

Later, we excitedly read the article written about them in the *New York Times* on June 5, 1868.

The public was greatly gratified not long ago to learn that this gallant English soldier had escaped his prison at the Dry Tortugas, and in his love of liberty at the risk of life, he had trusted himself to the mercies of a frail boat in an attempt to cross the Florida Straits to Cuba. We have the pleasure of stating that his voyage was made in safety, and that a letter has been received from him in Havana, sending his thanks and acknowledgements for kind treatment to some of the army officers at Tortugas, and stating that he was just about to sail for Old England. We do not doubt that every gentleman officer belonging to the garrison of his prison guard rejoices at his escape.

The "Lincoln conspirators" suffered because of the escapade of Grenfel and the others. We were again chained inside our cells and guarded even more closely than before. Because we were despondent, we remained silent about our newest abuse. I thought about Liberty and wondered if he missed George as much as I did.

Major Andrews did everything in his power to make our lives miserable. Our mail censorship became even tighter and was now handled by the Provost Marshal—an inquisitive and officious Yankee from Maine, who considered himself to be one of the elite, and daily added new rules to govern the prisoners. Our new regulations were more despotic than the laws of the ancient barbarians. If the Provost Marshal didn't like something in our letters he simply tore up the documents.

I sent one very important letter to Frank through a person heading for the mainland, but did not know for a long time whether she received it. I ended it with these words: *Hoping, my dearest Frank, our unhappy separation will soon end, and with it nothing to prevent the happiness we anticipate. I am, as ever, your devoted husband, SAM.*

31

May 30, 1868

The impeachment trial of President Johnson seems to be a farce. We try to read as much as we can about it in the newspapers, and occasionally someone will come to the island who is willing to sit down and discuss political news with those of us who are curious. We are not always correctly informed, and have often drawn erroneous conclusions. Now, with yet another change of commander, new regulations are in force. One of them is that all letters written and received are to be thoroughly examined, so we now receive them only after they have been opened and read.

My health continues to improve and our weather is finally quite pleasant in the shade. There is a good quantity of fresh tomatoes, peas, beans, collards and other tasty vegetables growing in the garden. The corn is in the silk and we look forward to roasting the ears.

We've not seen a newspaper for over a week now. I believe the new commanders (there are now two) are keeping them from us. The Provost Marshal seems to find delight in hiding any impeachment news from his prisoners. His prejudice is completely transparent through his words and his actions. But he will be leaving on furlough tomorrow, and we all look forward to a respite.

"Oh, how I miss those caustic discussions with Grenfel," I told Spangler and Arnold last night. "I long to discuss the impeachment proceedings with him."

"It will end as it was intended," said Ned. "The important thing for us to determine is: what will happen to us?"

"Ye of little faith," replied Samuel. "Once he's impeached, our unjust imprisonment will be resolved fairly and squarely." He sighed as he ran his hands through his hair.

"Are you not ever more weary and bitter about the tyranny and oppression?" Bitterness and hopeless grief had unfortunately become as familiar to me as our predictable food.

Our conversation was silenced by the arrival of the mail boat that would carry the Provost Marshal away with it. And another happy surprise lay in store: it delivered a pastor who would remain on the island for several days and hopefully share current news. I hurried to introduce myself and ask when he would offer a Christian service.

"Tomorrow morning, at 8:00 a.m. We shall meet after breakfast," he responded. "I hope to see you there."

Not only was I there, but I arrived early to ensure that Ned and Samuel would join me. They reluctantly agreed, assuming I had a trick up my sleeve.

His sermon was simple yet encouraging. We bowed our heads and prayed with Pastor McAfee, and then asked him if he could spare about ten minutes to speak with us privately. He nodded in understanding.

"Pastor McAfee, thank you for a very enlightening sermon," I began. "It means so much to us to be able to hear the Word."

Then I changed the subject with my most sincere smile. "There is assuredly some news on the President's impeachment and we would appreciate hearing about any of it."

I hoped my warm smile revealed my sincerity.

With half a smile he turned to face us. "How much do you know about what has transpired in the past month?"

"Very little," answered Ned. "They have taken away all newspapers and magazines because of our personal involvement and interest."

"You are the Lincoln conspirators, correct?" he asked sympathetically.

We nodded.

His eyes were kind. "Of course I will update you. Where should I start?"

We asked him to go back to the beginning of the month—when they took away our reading materials.

"Let me begin a little further back. You know that after suspending Secretary of War Stanton, President Johnson appointed General Grant to that position. This was unconstitutional because of the Tenure of Office Act of 1867, stating that a President may not dismiss important government officials without the permission of the Senate."

He paused and Samuel seized the moment. "So how could the President do that and get away with it?"

"The President defied the act. When Congress reconvened, they overruled Stanton's suspension and Grant resigned his position."

We looked at each other in wonder. These were details we did not know.

"However, once again President Johnson proceeded as he wished. Ignoring Congress, he again formally dismissed Secretary Stanton on February 21st. With the Republicans' support, Stanton responded by locking himself in his office and refusing to leave."

"I heard some of this from my wife, but by then our letters were being opened and read and she knew to no longer express her opinions about the political news," I said.

"Are you aware that the President was formally impeached by the House of Representatives on February 24th by a vote of 126 to 47? He was charged with violation of the Tenure of Office Act and bringing 'disgrace, ridicule, hatred, contempt and reproach to the Congress.'"

I shook my head. "But it's now in the Senate, correct?"

"Oh yes, it went to the Senate. That trial began on March 4th. It took eleven grueling weeks to finally come to a conclusion."

We nodded. Ned told the pastor we had been aware of the endless trial, but not the outcome.

"During the trial President Johnson made sure to be on his best behavior, impressing even his enemies. He promised to enforce the Reconstruction Acts and to abstain from giving speeches attacking Congress. Oh, and he also appointed a man well-liked by the Republicans, General John Schofield, as the new Secretary of War."

I listened and marveled at how knowledgeable and well-spoken the pastor was.

"Then, on May 16th, our President escaped removal from office by just one vote. He…"

"Just one vote? How is that possible?" I blurted.

"The votes were tallied and thirty-five Senators pronounced him guilty; nineteen pronounced him not guilty. Because two-thirds of the Senators did not find him guilty, Chief Justice Chase proclaimed that the President stood acquitted upon the articles of impeachment."

We sat in stunned silence. Now the facts had been laid out before us.

The three of us, friends and prisoners, looked from one another to Pastor McAfee. He chose to take a long moment before speaking.

"Is it truly possible you did not know the outcome?" he asked us.

"Yes, Sir. We are probably the last ones to know," I answered. "It was kept from us in spite, yet the Lord has brought you here to reveal the truth."

"Thank you for that," Samuel added, tears forming in his eyes. "It was time indeed."

Later that day I had time to compose a letter to Frank.

My dearest Frank:

No doubt your mind has been subject to many conjectures owing to my long silence. All letters are carefully perused by our Provost Marshal and due to his prying spirit and disposition to meddle with matters that do not pertain to his office, we are disinclined to send news home. I wish I did not have to pass this letter through his hands, and most likely, it will never reach you.

In the event that it does, we have been visited by a kind pastor who has updated us on the impeachment proceedings of the President. Because of this news, I

would like to know positively whether any action is con-
templated in my case between now and the fall election.
I am growing daily more bitter against tyranny and
oppression. Life often feels a burden to me, but for the
sake of you and the family I am restrained.
Your devoted husband,
SAM.

That night I slept peacefully, having finally learned the truth. I smiled, understanding that my renewed faith would give me the strength to continue fighting for my freedom.

32

November 20, 1868

Last August Spangler, Arnold and I paid a Key West attorney $100 each to obtain a federal court hearing, promising another $100 each if we were freed. There was no news from the Court until September 9th, when we learned that Judge Thomas J. Boynton had ruled that the previously mentioned "Milligan case" did not apply to us and our appeal was denied. In the Milligan case, the U.S. Supreme Court ruled that the federal government could not establish military courts to try civilians, except where civil courts were no longer functioning in an actual theatre of war. The Key West attorney did not collect his $300.

Two weeks ago I submitted my last official protest to Commander Hill regarding the boarding erected in front of our quarters. It had rendered our imprisonment "more painful and odious," I told him. We believed it was punishment based on secret information creditable to him. I asked for an investigation so that the truth be known. I am still awaiting his response.

We learned in July of John Surratt's release on bail, and the closing of his case. The Government's decision not to prosecute him can only be considered an official apology for his mother's unconscionable murder. Like the horse in the mire, the more they struggle to hide their bloody deeds, the deeper the officials in charge are sinking.

I cannot see the slightest justification for continuing to hold us, or comprehend the newspapers' unwillingness to question the legality of our imprisonment. We now believe that the judge in Key West was instructed not to grant the writ in our favor, since he gave us no logical or lawful reason for that decision.

Suffering so many disappointments has brought the three of us closer together and made us determined to not watch our tiny speck of hope flicker away. We have become extraordinarily aware of each other's moods, and constantly think of ways to improve them; one or the other is usually taking his turn in gloom and depression.

As a doctor I have always tried to prepare an effective medicine to treat my patients' physical ailments. Now I see that without the benefit of training, one or the other of my friends frequently becomes a "physician" and applies the proper treatment to keep us all from falling into deep despair.

This usually involves some form of physical activity and change of scenery.

"Let's go to the beach," Ned told Samuel and me shortly before dawn one morning. "I've just picked some good vegetables for Liberty."

He urged us up from our beds, which were actually no more than scraps of moss gathered from trees and pounded into hard mounds by our extensive and fitful usage.

"I'm in no mood to be miserable in the blazing sun," grumbled Samuel, pushing Ned's hand away.

I reached over and squeezed his shoulder. "Come along, Samuel. It's still early and the sun is just now rising. Anyway, what will you do here? There's nothing new to read, since you've read all the books in the library." I pulled out a letter from my waistband.

"Frank writes me to have courage just a while longer. She says, and I quote: '*The darkest hour is just before day, and our lives surely will not be a continual night. I truly believe President Johnson will release you before he goes out of office; and if he does not, I have assurance Grant will, so for my sake bear up a while longer, and God will send you safely home to me and our dear little children.*'"

I knew from her correspondence that she had spent two weeks in Baltimore searching for a man named Kerr, whom she understood was about to come to the Tortugas as the new commander. She was anxious to meet with him and provide him with copies of written documents. As it turned out, she had the wrong name and could not locate him. But her brother Jere was able to locate the new commander's father, who reassured him that his son was a good man who would not abuse our confidence or safety. So it seems we do have something to look forward to.

My appearance has significantly altered. I have shaved off my mustache and trimmed my goatee quite short. I scarcely know myself when I look in the glass. I cannot see many wrinkles or gray hairs, but my vision is not that good anymore. I know my hair is much thinner than when I left home. How will Frank perceive me after all this time? Knowing her, I don't believe it will make a difference. How I love her!

My mother is very ill and I cannot be certain I will see

her again. My spirts are so low I find myself unexpectedly weeping uncontrollably like a young girl without cause. The other conspirators tell me they experience the same emotional distress. How much fast-dwindling hope can one keep holding onto? We are being tested daily; it makes us even more desperate knowing that it is the same for our families.

The officials who have done us the most grievous damage are the slowest to right the wrong and provide suitable satisfaction. I have no confidence in their moral rectitude. I no longer believe that those who hold the ship of state will redress the grievances under which we suffer. Even though I am certain that while good begets more good, we all observe and suffer from the evil acts by those who have our lives in their hands. Those evil actions continue to compound to our detriment.

When we are mindful of some praiseworthy act performed by another person, our sense of love, honor, and esteem is immediately aroused. On the contrary, if insincerity or gross deception is practiced, then sentiments of anger, hatred and revenge result.

How earnestly I pray for us to be removed from this Hell on earth. Yet I am conscious that I need a promise from God in some form. I beseech Him each night to give me a positive sign before I lose the minimal strength derived from my faith, seemingly absent in my dark moments! Then I humbly ask for forgiveness and thank Him for keeping me going. The greatest resource I have, which came from Him, is the love I hold for Frank and my children.

Since our arrival I have been the only member of

our group to find solace in nightly prayers. The others respected my nightly murmuring ritual, but never joined in—until earlier this month. The depth of our despair and that sense of unity most likely led them to offer up prayers of their own in their personal words.

Although we continue to experience moments of hopelessness, expressing our faith gives us the capability to endure. Yet I continue to seek his strength: *Oh Lord, how much longer will you have me here? Please God, give me a sign to comprehend when this nightmare will come to an end.* Quivering with emotion I drop to the ground, welcoming the warm tears streaming down my cheeks.

33

March 10, 1869

War Department, Adjutant-General's Office
Washington, February 13, 1869

Commanding Officer
Fort Jefferson
Dry Tortugas, Florida

Sir: The Secretary of War directs that immediately on receipt of the official pardon, just issued by the President of the United States, in favor of Dr. Samuel A. Mudd, a prisoner now confined at Dry Tortugas, you release the said prisoner from confinement and permit him to go at large where he will.

You will please report the execution of this order and the date of departure of Dr. Mudd from the Dry Tortugas.

I am, sir, very respectfully your obdt. Servant,
E.D. Townsend
Assistant Adjutant-General

On February 13, 1869, President Johnson finally fulfilled his promise to Mrs. Mudd. Shortly before leaving the White House, he penned her a letter and sent it to her home by special messenger. The letter contained an invitation to come to the White House and accept Dr. Sam Mudd's pardon document.

Frank left for Washington immediately, but was detained on the way and did not reach the city until the following morning. She and Jere were received in the Executive Office of the White House by President Johnson.

"Good day, Mrs. Mudd. Good morning, Mr. Dyer. I hope you are both well," he began, smiling as he shook their hands. "Here are the papers for the release of Dr. Mudd," he added, handing Frank the large envelope.

"Thank you, Mr. President," she murmured through her tears. "Do you believe these papers can be sent safely through the mail?"

Both men noticed how the documents shook in her hands.

He smiled warmly, softening his facial features. "Mrs. Mudd, I will put the President's seal on them. I have complied with my promise to release your husband before I left the White House. I shall no longer hold myself responsible."

Jere spoke quietly. "We are deeply thankful for this large favor, Mr. President. I do have a question, however. Is there a possibility that the papers might go amiss—put away in some pigeonhole or corner?"

President Johnson shook his head and shrugged. "I should hope not, but there is always that possibility. Thus I prepared this copy of my letter to give you."

She smiled her thanks and offered him her hand. They

accepted the signed and sealed documents with relief and turned to go.

"Mrs. Mudd, I imagine you think this is tardy justice in carrying out my promise made to you two years ago." He paused a long moment. "I am truly sorry. The situation was such, however, that I could not act as I wanted to do."

They hurried outside to a nearby bench, where they sat down to open the envelope. It was a beautiful spring day: white and pink blossoms shimmered on the trees, while cheerful heads of daffodils danced with the tulips.

"Oh, Jere, I cannot believe he was finally given his freedom!" Frank exclaimed, embracing her brother. They broke out in a noisy, joyful laughter of relief and gratitude.

"I must take this to Sam at once," she told him, choking up. "I want to give it to him in person."

"Yes, you must travel to Baltimore straightaway and take the next steamer to the Dry Tortugas. I will return home and help care for your children."

Frank made haste to reach Baltimore, only to discover that the boat had departed just a few hours earlier. She broke down in tears after learning that the next steamer would not be leaving for two or three weeks.

She then made the decision to send the papers by express to Thomas O. Dyer, her brother in New Orleans, and asked him to pay Mr. Loutrel $300 to deliver them to Fort Jefferson.

* * *

So I had been a free man for nearly a month before I heard about it. When the pardon reached me on March 8th, this personal letter was attached.

Headquarters, Fort Jefferson, Fla
March 8, 1869
Special Order No. 42:

In obedience to communication from War Depart-
ment A.G. Office, Washington, D.C., dated February
13, 1869, Dr. Samuel A. Mudd (a prisoner) is hereby
released from confinement and permitted to go at large
where he will.

By order Brevt. Major General Hunt
J.M. Lancaster
Brevt. Capt. U.S.A., 1st Lieut. 3rd Artillery, Adjutant

The news knocked the breath out of me like a sudden
Caribbean squall. I stumbled to a stone bench outside the
commander's office. I said nothing to the prisoners chatting with each other nearby; my two closest friends were
still waiting to receive their pardons and I wanted to share
the news of my pardon privately.

I found them pitching pennies against our outside
wall. I took a huge breath and walked over to them.
When they turned to me, I gradually shared the contents
of my letter.

Ned tossed his coins into the air with a cackling Rebel
yell. Samuel grabbed me in a crushing embrace. "You are
white as snow," he exclaimed, studying my face.

"Thank you for celebrating with me, Ned and Samuel. And your celebration will not be long in coming. Mr.
Loutrel has heard that your pardons are on their way."

My friends beamed with genuine happiness. Our

embraces were strong and heartfelt. Some of the other prisoners walked over, and we showed them the pardon.

"Praise the Lord!" shouted Ned. "All those prayers and Bible readings were heard! And you deserve to be the first to leave!"

(Three weeks after I left Fort Jefferson their letters of pardon reached them. By then I was at home with my family and we celebrated the wonderful news with prayers of thanksgiving.)

There was one piece of unfinished business to attend to before leaving for home: locating a new caretaker for Liberty who would appreciate the gravity of this charge.

Most people on the island would likely consider the care and feeding of a humble, once-wild sea creature a bother. They would not comprehend how capably that sturdy shell had borne the pain, hopes and constant struggles of Grenfel and myself.

I walked into the kitchen to speak with a cook who had always treated us kindly.

Jacob was chopping vegetables while humming contentedly to himself.

"Jacob, you know about Liberty, right?"

"I know him. He knows me. I sometimes take him bits of vegetables and fruits when I remember."

After I told him my request, he picked up a handful of vegetable scraps. We walked together ceremoniously to "pass on the tortoise shell," so to speak. This would be my farewell walk to the far corner of the island.

Liberty came lumbering out of his quarters before we reached him, after hearing the sound of our voices. I believe his sharp and intuitive mind realized that something was changing.

I told him anyway, voicing the message in my own words. "Liberty, ol' boy, first Grenfel, now me. Leaving you is hard, but Jacob here will watch out for you, and you know how to survive anyhow." I squatted next to him and reached over to scratch his head.

"I will miss you, but now I'm free and will be reunited with my family." Wiping away a stray tear, I added, "Go make a family as well, Liberty. I think you deserve that happiness too."

Liberty solemnly dipped his head before emitting that unmistakable gulp, as if agreeing to the new arrangement. When Jacob reached down to scratch his leathery head, he was thanked with another gulp to call his own.

"He does know you, friend. I feel good about turning him over to you."

Jacob laughed. "He will welcome anyone who brings him food. He knows he's a pet, but I think he also knows he could do right fine on his own."

As we stood up, I turned to Liberty one last time. "Cheerio, good bloke, as Grenfel would say." A combination of momentary regret and deep satisfaction washed over me.

I had made my peace with God, and was eager and grateful to be going home. My long ordeal was over. I had been in government custody just six weeks shy of four years, from April 21, 1865, when I was arrested at the farm, until March 8, 1869, when my pardon letter arrived. As a free man, now with all liberties available, I was forced to wait three more days for the ship to carry me home.

34

MARCH 30, 1869

On March 11th I boarded the Navy schooner *Matchless* for the short journey to Key West. From its deck, I was given a final glimpse of my prison fortress for the first time as a free man. The sun was up and the sky was an empty, clear blue. I would drink the sky if I could, drink it and celebrate it and let it fill me up.

With childish glee, I raised both hands and waved goodbye to the two lighthouses: the one on Garden Key and the taller one on Loggerhead Key. The tropical trees I had so often walked among as a prisoner now seemed to be trading farewells with our vessel—a restful sight to my tired eyes. I focused on the shifting motion of the gentle waves caressing the walls of the moat and my thoughts turned to Liberty. Was he somewhere under those trees watching us depart? Perhaps preparing to leave the island to pursue new adventures?

As the islands became mere specks on the horizon, my unforgettable friend Colonel George Grenfel seemed to be standing alongside me waving to his sea turtle friend. I might never know if Grenfel had found freedom—and could only ardently wish that he would know that I had.

Arriving at Key West, I quickly secured passage on

the steamship *Liberty* that had just arrived from Havana, with holds full of sugar, tropical fruit, and cases of Cuban cigars. Normally a pipe smoker, my new life seemed to call for a special celebration; when offered a Cuban cigar I gratefully accepted and enjoyed it!

The *Liberty* docked in Baltimore on March 18th. I rested for one day in Jere's home before taking my short ride home. During that brief time, I gratefully greeted my friends and prominent Marylanders who stopped by to welcome me back. Some of them had worked hard for my release, including Governor Oden Bowie.

And then, after almost four years of being forced to deal with a bizarre new situation and so many harsh realities, my perpetual dream came true. On March 20th I walked into the sunlight streaming through my own front window and fell at last into my beloved's welcoming arms.

Frank was as lovely as I remembered her, although noticeably thinner. Like me, gray hairs mingled with her darker curls. Her adoring face had become etched with fine lines during four difficult years spent caring for our farm and family. She was such a beautiful sight.

Her lips were warm and sweet against mine; we held each other even more tightly than on the day I had been taken away. Despite all the pain and self-doubt of the past we steadfastly acknowledged, we were now ready to make the most of our new beginning. At that moment, the years of our separation seemed to melt away.

I searched her soft and tender eyes. There was one burning question I needed to ask. "And Mama?"

She shook her head. "She's gone, Sammy. She tried to

wait for you, but her heart gave out. She told me to tell you how much she loved you."

I stood perfectly still as the grief spread slowly through me. Then I asked fearfully, "Is Papa well?"

This time she smiled briefly. "He's doing fine, strong as ever. But he misses her so." She laughed lightly. "Now that he has you back it will give him a reason to live."

The children were shy with me, as was to be expected. But they allowed me to kneel before them and gently gather each one into my arms as I spoke to them in a soft voice. I am certain they could feel my bony body through my clothing, which probably frightened them as well. I proceeded slowly over the next few days, giving them the time they needed to get to know me again.

Frank and I moved out to the porch to get reacquainted. Her blue eyes were soft and calm as we tenderly studied each other. I loved the familiar way she held her head, the fading sunlight illuminating her profile, and the delicate lines of her cheek and pulsing throat. She lifted my hand in hers, and as I felt the thrill of her touch I sensed my body unwinding; ready for anything.

Facing her, I stroked her hair back from her face. "I do feel quite fortunate, Frankie. My four children, my wife and my father are here with me. My medical practice awaits me and the farm craves my attention."

Her eyes dropped as her face clouded over. "Oh Sam, the farm is in a terrible state. We've no laborers to cultivate it; the fences have fallen down; other buildings need repair; and money is almost unattainable."

After prison such concerns no longer troubled me and I quickly reassured her. "We will survive this together. We have suffered through so much already, and with God's help we can overcome every tribulation."

She looked into my eyes and smiled with her whole being. Hand in hand, we walked into the kitchen, where I gladly helped her prepare our first supper together.

* * *

On March 1, 1869, three weeks after my pardon, President Johnson pardoned the other two conspirators. Those who have studied our case generally agree that Ned Spangler had nothing to do with the assassination of President Lincoln. But, always the philosophical one, Ned used to tell me and the others at Fort Jefferson: "They made a mistake by sending me down here. I had nothing to do with Booth or the assassination of President Lincoln; but I suppose I have done enough in my life to deserve this, so I shall make the best of it."

Samuel Arnold's father traveled to Fort Jefferson to bring his son back home. Samuel, his father, and Spangler journeyed back to Baltimore together on the steamship *Cuba. The Baltimore Sun* of April 7, 1869 reported their arrival.

Local Matters: Return of Arnold and Spangler, the Dry Tortugas Prisoners—*Samuel B. Arnold and Edman Spangler, the prisoners recently released from the Dry Tortugas, under pardon of President Johnson, the former having been sentenced for life and the latter for six years, by the military commission that tried the assassination conspirators, reached this city yesterday. They came as passengers on the steamship Cuba, from*

Key West. Arnold appears in rather delicate health, but Spangler is well, and both seem in good spirits. They are set free now, after three years and eight months in confinement.

After their trial and sentence, they reached the Dry Tortugas with Dr. Mudd, their late fellow-prisoner, and Michael O'Laughlen, who died during imprisonment on the 24th of July, 1865, and were released on the 22nd of March 1869. They received a telegram on the 9th of March, informing them of their pardon. Spangler says it appeared to him that from that time until the 21st, when Arnold's father reached there with the pardons, he gained in flesh every hour. Arnold was employed as a clerk at headquarters and Spangler as a carpenter, and both at times were compelled to work very hard.

On the terrible ordeal of the trial, under the circumstances by which they were surrounded, it is not to be supposed they would delight to dwell. Spangler says that from the torture he endured he was mostly unconscious of the proceedings in the case, and often knew nothing of what was going on around him. When the padded hood was placed upon his head in prison, covering over his eyes and tightened about his neck and chest, with manacles already on both hands and feet, he was told it was by order of Secretary Stanton, the subordinate thus excusing himself for the action. After arriving at the Fort, and up to the time of his release, Spangler claims that the sense of his entire innocence only made his chains more galling, whilst at the same time it often kept him from utter despair. Both Arnold and Spangler speak of the kindness and attention they received on board the Cuba *from Capt. Dukehart, his officers and passengers, who generally were disposed to make them comfortable.*

Several weeks later, Frank walked from the kitchen out to the back yard and discovered a man roosting in a tree.

She shouted up to him. "Who are you? What are you doing up there?"

Ned grinned pleasantly, despite his unseemly position.

"Good Day, Mrs. Mudd. I am Ned Spangler, a friend of your husband."

"Why are you up the tree?" she asked incredulously.

"I asked someone to tell me the way to Dr. Mudd's farm and followed the road. When I got here, your dogs chased me right up here," he explained sheepishly.

"Oh my. Well, they are far down the field now, so come on down," she told him, hands on hips and heart filled with laughter.

He slowly made his way down the tree while Frank shouted for me to come out.

"What an honor to be rescued yet again by my best friend," he laughed as I hurried through the back door. "After years feeling certain you could not get along without me, it was I needing a rescue!" We threw our arms around each other.

I had thought my prospects for happiness could not improve. Ned's arrival and buoyant spirits proved me wrong. "I told you we would celebrate your freedom together!"

After a breakfast filled with laughter and happy memories, Ned and I discussed his future. Feeling we should always be together, he asked permission to build a shed on my property and live there. He would repay his keep with farm and carpentry work. Knowing he was now all alone, this seemed like a most sensible plan. Both Frank and I welcomed him to live with us.

Ned quickly constructed a little place to live on our property. Looking ahead, I decided to gift him five acres of land so he could build his own home. We were all happy to have him with us. He played games with our children and they adored him. My oldest son Andrew described him as "a quiet, genial man, greatly respected by the members of our family and the people of the neighborhood."

In my mind, Ned would always be one of the angels who saved my life.

As my medical practice resumed, it became painfully obvious how impoverished my neighbors had become since the war. I provided medical treatment free of charge if they could not pay. In any case, rebuilding and maintaining the farm had also become more than I could handle and Ned's cheerful and efficient help became invaluable.

As the days passed, I became aware of the many friends throughout the countryside who believed in my innocence and spoke well of us. They told me they knew we would be vindicated one day.

The day Frank told me we were expecting our fifth child, I burst into unexpected tears.

"I am delighted to hear that, my love. God continues to bless us. What shall we name him?'

She laughed gleefully. "Him? We already have three boys. Don't you think another girl would be wonderful company for little Lillian?"

I pulled her close. "Of course I do. And we shall give

her a little sister or two. We have time. But this one, little Henry, is very much a boy," I whispered. "He will arrive strong and happy because his family's history is so resilient."

My prediction proved correct and little Henry joined our growing family less than a year after my return, healthy and boisterous.

Frank was also prophetic. We were blessed with three more daughters over the years: Stella Marie Mudd, Rose De Lima "Ernie" Mudd, and Mary Eleanor "Nettie" Mudd, as well as one more son, Edward Joseph Mudd.

My steadfast family and faith carried me through to a blessed ending and a joyful new beginning.

As the good Word says: *Our cups runneth over.*

EPILOGUE

Samuel and Frank Mudd looked forward to many years of peace and happiness together. They welcomed five more children and proudly celebrated one son as he earned his medical degree and their daughter's choice to become a nun. But tragedies were waiting to strike.

Their son Henry, born the year after Sam's release from prison, died eight months after his birth. Sam's father passed away in 1877, and their firstborn son Andrew in 1882, at the age of twenty-four. His best friend Ned Spangler succumbed to the lasting effects of imprisonment two years later without finishing his home on the Mudd property. He was buried at St. Peter's Cemetery in the Mudd family plot, just two miles from the five farm acres he had been so proud to call his own.

Samuel Arnold, the last of the "conspirator prisoners," returned to the Baltimore area and lived out of the public eye for more than thirty years. In 1902, he wrote a series of articles for the *Baltimore American* newspaper describing his imprisonment at Fort Jefferson. He often complained that he was still the subject of much hatred for something he had not done. Arnold died four years later on September 21, 1906. He is buried at Green Mount Cemetery in Baltimore, Maryland. Michael O'Laughlen, who died of yellow fever at Fort Jefferson, is also buried at Green Mount Cemetery.

With Arnold's death, the only main figure in the Lincoln Assassination story still alive was John H. Surratt Jr., who died on April 21, 1916, at the age of seventy-two. He is buried in the New Cathedral Cemetery in Baltimore, Maryland.

Dr. Mudd was pardoned, but never forgiven. He and his family were still targets of threats and verbal abuse. He could restore the farm, which had fallen into disrepair, but never his reputation. Many former patients switched to other doctors.

Dr. Mudd remained active in community affairs. In 1874 he was elected Chief Officer of the local Farmers' Association called the Bryantown Grange. He became Vice-President of the local Democratic Tilden-Hendricks Presidential election committee in 1876, where Tilden lost to Republican Rutherford B. Hayes in a hotly disputed election. The following year Sam ran as a Democratic candidate for the position of delegate in the Maryland State Legislature, but lost in the primary election to Samuel Cox, Jr., whose foster father had helped hide Booth and Herold for five days after they left the Mudd farm in their escape to Virginia.

Two years later several of his good friends, hoping to boost his morale, nominated him as the Republican candidate for a local office in Charles County. But they had apparently forgotten that it was the Republican Party that sent him to prison. Sam considered the nomination "a bad joke" and would have nothing to do with it.

In 1878, the same year his ninth child Mary Eleanor "Nettie" was born, he and Frank temporarily took in a seven-year-old orphan named John Burke, one of the three hundred abandoned children sent to Maryland families from the New York City Foundling Asylum run by the Catholic Sisters of Charity. The little boy was soon permanently settled with farmer Ben Jenkins.

In 1880, the *Port Tobacco Times* reported that the Mudd

farm barn, containing almost eight thousand pounds of tobacco, two horses, a wagon, and farm implements was destroyed by fire.

During his final years, he dedicated himself to his family and his medical practice. Once again, in a paradoxical twist of fate, it proved to be his undoing. On New Year's Day of 1883, Dr. Mudd rode out into the cold, rainy night to tend to one of his patients. Returning home and shaking with fever, he climbed upstairs to his bedroom and shut himself in. By the next morning he knew he had pneumonia, but there was no one nearby to give him medical attention other than Frank, who nursed him as best she could. He seemed to know his time had come and quietly succumbed nine days later, on January 10, 1883. He was forty-nine years old. His youngest daughter Nettie turned five that day.

Dr. Mudd was given a prominent plot in St. Mary's Catholic Church Cemetery in Bryantown, Maryland. Ironically, that was the site of his first meeting with John Wilkes Booth nineteen years before.

His beloved Sarah Frances Dyer Mudd lived a much longer life, and remained close to her seven children to share their trials and joys. She passed away in 1911, at the age of seventy-six, and is buried next to her husband in St. Mary's Catholic Church Cemetery in Bryantown, Maryland.

Dr. Samuel Mudd's fame did not die with him. Having suffered countless indignations, taunts, jeers and mean-spirited accusations, his seven children were determined to prove him innocent. With each passing year, President Lincoln's fame grew in stature while anyone associated with his death was condemned to go down in history as another Benedict Arnold.

Dr. Mudd's third oldest son, Dr. Thomas Dyer Mudd, chose to seek solace with his wife in a haunted house in the Anacostia section of Washington. There he lost his wife to illness after she had borne him five children. He remarried five years later but his brooding became darker and darker until he died in 1929. None of the family ever remembered him mentioning the Lincoln assassination.

In 1936, Twentieth-Century Pictures adapted the story, written by his daughter Nettie, into a movie based on his imprisonment entitled *The Prisoner of Shark Island*. This became a classic and was directed by John Ford, written by Nunnally Johnson and starred Warner Baxter.

Suddenly, Samuel Mudd changed from a villain into a great American folk hero. During the next two decades, ten radio and television specials were aired, a grade school was named after him, a hospital room was dedicated to him and Congress inaugurated a memorial to him at Fort Jefferson.

Three family members were responsible for this reversal of fortune. His youngest daughter Nettie's collection of her father's correspondence to Frank and others brought the world a firsthand description of her father's story. Frank Mudd's memories of their times together put the letters in context and brought his story to vivid life. And Dr. Richard Dyer Mudd, son of the moody Dr. Tom, vowed to spend the rest of his life saving his grandfather's reputation.

When he graduated from Georgetown University with a master's degree in sociology, a doctorate in history, and a doctorate in medicine, he moved to Michigan. There he wrote a family genealogy. On weekends and vacations, he toured the country, educating historical societies and schools about the life of his famous ancestor. He visited thirty-five states, the District of Columbia, three foreign countries, and the Virgin Islands on this quest.

Under great pressure from Dr. Richard Mudd and others, Congress passed a bill in 1959 creating a monument to honor Sam at Fort Jefferson. But that was not enough. The family wanted someone in authority to declare that Samuel Mudd had been "an innocent man who was unreasonably sent to prison."

The White House was bombarded with resolutions, petitions and letters from more than three dozen Senators and Congressmen, calling for Dr. Mudd's exoneration. Even seven states' legislatures passed resolutions and sent them to the White House.

On July 24, 1979, President Jimmy Carter wrote a two-page letter stating that he was legally unable to overturn the conviction, yet his opinion regarding Dr. Mudd's innocence was that it should be overturned. *"I hope my opinion restores dignity to your grandfather's name and clears the Mudd family name of any negative connotation or implied lack of honor."*

Television anchorman Roger Mudd—a distant relative of Sam's—and other members of the news corps gave President Carter's letter international coverage. Eight years later President Ronald Reagan wrote another letter in response to one received from Dr. Richard Dyer Mudd. *"Believe me, I'm truly sorry I can do nothing to help you in your long crusade. In my efforts to help, I came to believe as you do that Dr. Samuel Mudd was indeed innocent of any wrongdoing."*

Reagan's participation in what was now being called "the crusade" brought others to the table, like George McNarmara, a dynamic Philadelphia investment banker. He approached his congressional contacts, especially Senator Joseph R. Biden, Jr. of Delaware, and asked them to convince the Secretary of the Army to re-open Sam's case. The case was eventually presented to the high-ranking group of civilian employees called the Army Board for Correction of Military Records, chaired by Charles A. Chase, a great-grandnephew of former Supreme Court Chief Justice Salmon P. Chase.

The five-man panel met on January 22, 1992 at the Pentagon, with reporters, attorneys and members of the Mudd family. Nine witnesses were sworn in and the opening statement was made by Dr. Mudd's great-grandson, Richard J. Mudd of Virginia.

The attorneys discussed the legality of bringing civilian defendants before an Army tribunal during peacetime. One of the attorneys was Candida Ewing Staempfli Steel, the great-great-granddaughter of Dr. Mudd's original attorney, General Thomas Ewing. The testimony at the original trial of Dr. Mudd was discussed in detail, drawing the final conclusion that the government had completely failed to prove its case against Dr. Mudd for either plotting to kill the president or consciously helping Booth to escape.

More testimonies were given. Dr. John K. Lattimer, a medical researcher and author, cited the physicians' obligations under the Hippocratic Oath to treat those in need of medical attention. He then added the vital information that Dr. Mudd had given to the soldiers looking for Booth.

Laura Chappelle, a great-great-granddaughter of Dr. Mudd and an appellate attorney, testified regarding the legal limitations placed on Dr. Mudd and General Ewing, which made it nearly impossible to present an adequate defense. Dr. Mudd had been denied a trial by jury, the advice of legal counsel until the day before the trial began, and an opportunity to testify in his own defense.

The closing speaker was the man whose lifetime dream had come down to this sudden-death hearing: Dr. Richard D. Mudd, who was now ninety-two years old. He thanked everyone for making the hearing possible and ended the day with these words: "I hope this hearing will permit my grandfather and grandmother to rest in peace."

All five members of the Army Board for Correction of Military Records agreed that Dr. Mudd's trial had been a terrible miscarriage of justice, and the Archivist of the United States was ordered to set aside the conviction. However, an acting Assistant Secretary of the Army disagreed, stating that the board was not in the business of settling historical disputes. Knowing the board had intervened in a number of other historic cases in the past, the Mudd family appealed this ruling.

In 1993, there was a mock trial at the University of Richmond. Three prestigious judges stated that Dr. Mudd's conviction had flagrantly violated the American Constitution. The defense team representing Dr. Mudd included F. Lee Bailey, one of the best-known attorneys in the United States.

The Army, after years of study, still refused to change its mind. The case was taken by Attorney Steel to federal court in the District of Columbia. In October 1998, Judge Paul L. Friedman ruled that the Army had acted "arbitrarily and capriciously" in denying the Mudd family appeal and ordered military officials to reconsider their position.

The Army would not reconsider and by the end of 2000 the case was back in federal court. Dr. Richard D. Mudd, now ninety-four years old, spoke up again. "If the courts refuse to clear my grandfather's name, the case will be carried forward by my children, my grandchildren, my great-grandchildren and my great-great-grandchildren."

Sadly, it was not to be. When it finally reached the Supreme Court for consideration in 2003, they refused to take the case, stating the Mudd family's attorney had "missed the deadline for filing the case." That error, by the Mudd's Washington D.C. attorney, snuffed out the last hope of his descendants to overturn the conviction.

"It's heartbreaking to lose this way," said Thomas B. Mudd of Saginaw, Michigan, the doctor's great-grandson and plaintiff in the case.

"We never held out great hope that the Supreme Court would do justice for Dr. Mudd, but to not even get the case in front of them after all this time is truly hard to take."

The lawyer's error put an unexpected and unsatisfying end to the quest begun in the 1930's by the late Dr. Richard D. Mudd. Even those who thought that Dr. Samuel Mudd played a larger role in the Lincoln assassination are not satisfied with the result. There will always be an element of doubt. There will never be that final judicial closure.

ACKNOWLEDGMENTS

Once again, I want to give endless thanks to my book team. Every one of them gave me the guidance, patience and kindness that was so essential to see me through this project. Very special thanks go to Carey "Trip" Giudici and Cathy Drury, who tackled the challenging task of co-editing this story. Both of you truly understood what I wanted to say, and then provided me with "better words" when needed.

To Patty Osborne, my genius friend who takes the manuscripts and covers and transforms them into beautiful books, I want to thank you for coming out of retirement to work with me again. This is the twelfth book we've collaborated on together, and I'm certain it won't be the last.

To my proof readers, all of whom worked overtime, you offered me wisdom and encouragement. Suzi Hassel, Diane Knight and Cassandra Coveney, thank you so much. You've all worked with me in the past and have become an important part of my writing family.

I am once again grateful and indebted to my dear friend and cover artist Gini Steele, who has produced the "perfect cover" for my last five books. A heartfelt thank you for your lovely work as well as your camaraderie.

To Buddy Sullivan, Coastal Georgia historian, my friend and award-winning author, I thank you for your encouragement and guidance. You are never too busy to answer my questions and read my manuscripts. I am so very grateful to you.

There were many primary sources, books, essay, letters

and articles about Dr. Samuel Mudd's life that became the bedrock of my research. A special shout-out goes to Donna Peterson and Eddie Roberts, who met Mike and me at the Mudd Farm in Maryland (on the day it was closed to the public) and toured us through the rooms, the grounds, the farmland, and John Wilkes Booth's escape route through the Zekiah Swamp. Both of these new friends were extremely gracious in sharing their time and knowledge with us.

After visiting the Dry Tortugas and Fort Jefferson, I contacted the Chief Ranger of the Everglades Mike Michener, who answered my many questions and then referred me to John Fuechsel—Park Ranger and Interpreter of the Dry Tortugas National Park. John sent me some of his photos of the fort—one which appears on the cover of this book. He also put me into contact with Ms. Allyson Gantt, Chief of Public Affairs, who provided information and answered more questions. Thank you to each one of you for your invaluable assistance.

I owe my family so much for their unending patience and encouragement. To my wonderful unflappable daughters—Cassandra and Ticiana—many thanks and much love to you both. To my beloved mother Phyllis, thank you for your loving support and critique of my work. And I thank God you are just a phone call away when I need to talk.

My profound whole-hearted thanks go to my husband Michael: so wise, warm, generous and steadfast with his unconditional faith in me and my work. He listened to me as I recounted the challenges and joys of writing this novel and he never let up in his encouragement. As with every book I write, I looked to him for support and laughter. His love sustained me every day. His confidence in me was an additional bonus.

And to my Heavenly Father—what can I say that You don't already know? Thank you for your grace—and for never letting me go.

BOOK GROUP DISCUSSION QUESTIONS

1. Could you relate to Dr. Mudd? Did you feel compassion for him? Did your feelings toward him change by the time you finished the book?

2. Dr. Samuel Mudd is a flawed character. Were his actions understandable in light of his fear for his family's safety?

3. The paradox of injustice reigns throughout this story. How can something judged wrongly weigh us down so much? Discuss.

4. How did you feel about the prisoners' friendships? Did they evolve in their own ways? What do you think they learned from their shared experiences and from one another in this true story?

5. Grief is an important theme of the book. Were Dr. Mudd's reactions to his circumstances understandable?

6. What impact does the relationship with some of the Lincoln conspirators have on Samuel Mudd?

7. Do you think Samuel Mudd made the right decision when he admitted to having met John Wilkes Booth? What decision would you have made in his place?

8. Several of the characters in this novel suffered because of the decisions they made. Discuss the themes of guilt, grief and redemption in this story.

9. Is forgiveness an important theme in this story? If so, how? Is forgiveness something you do for someone else, or for yourself?

10. Throughout the novel, Dr. Mudd describes himself as feeling as if he were watching his life from the outside. What do you think he is trying to convey here?

11. On the surface, Dr. Mudd's and Colonel Grenfel's lives couldn't have been more different. In what ways are their stories similar?

12. What role does his faith play during Dr. Mudd's incarceration?

13. How was Dr. Mudd able to cope with the consequences of being imprisoned for almost four years?

14. How does Dr. Mudd grow or change as a character throughout the story? How does he stay the same?

15. How was Dr. Mudd able to cope with the consequences of being imprisoned for almost four years?

RESOURCES

Primary Sources

McHale, John E. Jr., *Dr. Samuel A. Mudd and the Lincoln Assassination,* Westminster, MD, Heritage Books, 2007.

Mudd, Nettie, *The Life of Dr. Samuel A. Mudd*, New York, NY, The Neale Publishing Company, 1906.

O'Reilly, Bill, *Killing Lincoln: The Shocking Assassination That Changed America Forever,* New York, NY, Henry Hold and Company, 2011.

Steers, Edward, Jr., *His Name Is Still Mudd: The Case Against Dr. Samuel Alexander Mudd,* Gettysburg, PA, Thomas Publications, 1997.

Summers, Robert K., *Get The Doctor From His Cell: Samuel Mudd, Yellow Fever, and Redemption Behind Bars,* Arlington, VA, Create Space Independent Publishing, 2015.

Secondary Sources

Angel, Paul, *The Lincoln Reader,* New Brunswick, Canada, Rutgers University Press, 1947.

Barr, Nevada, *Flashback,* Waterville, ME, G.P. Putnam's Sons, 2003.

Bishop, Jim, *The Day Lincoln Was Shot,* New York, NY, Harper and Brothers, 1955.

Carter, Samuel, III, *The Riddle of Dr. Mudd,* New York, NY, Putman, 1974.

Chamlee, Roy A., *Lincoln's Assassins: A Complete Account of Their Capture, Trial, and Punishment*, Nashville, TN, McFarland & Company, 1990.

Forrester, Izola, *This One Mad Act: The Unknown Story of John Wilkes Booth and his Family*, Boston, MA, Cushman & Flint, 1937.

Hanchett, William, *The Lincoln Murder Conspiracy,* Urbana, IL, University of Illinois Press, 1983.

Higdon, Hal, *The Union vs. Dr. Mudd,* Chicago, IL, Follett Publishing, 1964.

Jones, John Paul, ed., *Dr. Mudd and the Lincoln Assassination: The Case Re-opened,* Conshohocken, PA, Combined Books, 1995.

Kauffmann, Michael W. ed., *Samuel Bland Arnold: Memoirs of a Lincoln Conspirator,* Bowie, MD, Heritage Press, 1997.

Kauffmann, Michael W., *In The Footsteps Of An Assassin,* Travel Brains, 2012.

Landrum, Wayne L., *Fort Jefferson and the Dry Tortugas National Park,* Big Pine Key, FL., 2003.

Manuey, Albert C., *Pages From The Past: A Pictorial History of Fort Jefferson,* Literary License, 2014.

Pitman, Ben, *The Assassination of President Lincoln and the Trial of the Conspirators,* Create Space Independent Publishing, 2012.

Surratt Society, *From War Department Files: Statements Made by the Alleged Lincoln Conspirators Under Examination 1865,* Clinton, MD, 1980.

Weckesser, Elden C., *His Name Was Mudd: The Life of Dr. Samuel A. Mudd, Who Treated The Fleeing John Wilkes Booth,* Jefferson. N.C., McFarland & Co., 1991.

Weichmann, Louis J., *A True History of the Assassination of Abraham Lincoln and the Conspiracy of 1865,* New York, NY, Alfred A. Knopf, 1975.

Blogs and Magazine Articles

Dry Tortugas-Fort Jefferson, www.travelyesplease.com/travel-blog-dry-tortugas-fort-jefferson/

Farley, M. Foster, *George St. Leger Grenfell: British Soldier of Fortune,* Confederate Veteran Magazine, Vol. II, 1996.

Higdon, Hal, *On the Trail of Dr. Mudd,* 2011.

Holden, Emily, *At the Dry Tortugas During the War,* www.fcit.usf.edu.

O'Donaghue, Alfred, *"Thirty Months at the Dry Tortugas"*, Galaxy Magazine, February 1869, Vol. 7, Issue 2.

Olasky, Marilyn, *Pilgrim Politician*, World Magazine, February 16, 2008.

Pot of Gold, https://potogold.wordpress.com/dry-tortugas-trip

Internet Articles

Abandoned on a Desert Island, Shannon Tech, www.shannontech.com/ParkVision/DryTortugas/html.

Dr. Samuel A. Mudd-American History, Confederacy, www.historynet.com/dr-samuel-a-mudd. 6/12/2006.

Dr. Samuel Mudd, http://roger.jnorton.com/lincoln29.

Dr. Samuel A. Mudd/History Net: Where History Comes Alive-World & U.S. History Online/From the World's Largest History Magazine Publisher, www.historynet.com/dr-samuel-a-mudd.htm.

Dry Tortugas (Loggerhead Key) FL, www.lighthousefriends.com

Dry Tortugas National Park, www.travel.nationalgeographic.com/travel/nationaol.parks/dry-tortugas-national-park.

Dry Tortugas, https://en.wikipidia.org/wiki/drytortugas

George St. Leger Grenfell, www.wikipedia.com

History & Ecology of Mangroves in the Dry Tortugas, T.W. Doyle, http: www.hwrc.gov

Long, Kat, *The Assassination of Abraham Lincoln-How Samuel Mudd Went From Lincoln Conspirator to Medical Savior,* Special Report, Smithsonian, www.smithsonianmag.com/history/how-samuel-mudd-went-lincoln-conspirator-medicalsavior/History/Smithsonian.

National Geographic Travel, Dry Tortugas National Park, http://travel.nationalgeographic.com/travel/national-park/dry-tortugas.

St. Leger Grenfell, Krick, *Confederate Staff Officers with Ohio Connections,* www.cincinnatiwrt.org/data/articles/Krick.

The Assassin's Doctor, Dr. Samuel A. Mudd Research Site, www.samuelmudd.com.

The Escape Attempt of Dr. Mudd, Harper's Weekly on line, www.boothiebarn.files.wordpress.com/2012/03/dr-mudds-attempted-escape-a-harpers-weekly.jpg.

We Lived Here Too, Surratt House Museum, www.surratt.org

ABOUT THE ARTIST

Combining her mutual love of photography and history, Gini Steele and her husband Richard have created an extensive collection of photographic images of times long gone by. Throughout their work with historical societies, archivists and researchers they realized that there was a need to restore and reproduce these historic images and make  them available before they are lost forever.

Staying true to the genre, Ms. Steele used traditional photographic processes to both restore and reproduce the collection of old glass plates, negatives and photographs. She enjoys the challenge of interpreting the old negatives in her darkroom and prints the silver gelatin photographs by hand one at a time. Once the photographs are printed, they are tinted by hand. Once the hand-tinting is accomplished, Gini uses digital technology to complete the image, creating a unique piece of art.

Gini resides in Beaufort, SC with her two cats Bailey and Penelope Butterbeans.